SANS DOCTEUR
HOSPITAL

ANNE C. SMITH

SANS DOCTEUR
HOSPITAL

TATE PUBLISHING
AND ENTERPRISES, LLC

Sans Docteur Hospital
Copyright © 2013 by Anne C. Smith. All rights reserved.

No part of this publication may be reproduced, stored in a retrieval system or transmitted in any way by any means, electronic, mechanical, photocopy, recording or otherwise without the prior permission of the author except as provided by USA copyright law.

The opinions expressed by the author are not necessarily those of Tate Publishing, LLC.

Published by Tate Publishing & Enterprises, LLC
127 E. Trade Center Terrace | Mustang, Oklahoma 73064 USA
1.888.361.9473 | www.tatepublishing.com

Tate Publishing is committed to excellence in the publishing industry. The company reflects the philosophy established by the founders, based on Psalm 68:11,
"The Lord gave the word and great was the company of those who published it."

Book design copyright © 2013 by Tate Publishing, LLC. All rights reserved.
Cover design by Matias Alasagas
Interior design by Jomel Pepito

Published in the United States of America

ISBN: 978-1-62147-834-8
1. Fiction / Suspense
2. Fiction / Romance / General
12.12.11

Dedication

This book is dedicated to all of the wonderful people with whom I have had the opportunity to work during my long career in healthcare. Although my book portrays the dark side of the medical profession, it is purely fictional. The vast majority of nurses and physicians I have met over the years are kind, caring, and dedicated professionals, and it has been an honor and a pleasure to work with them.

Acknowledgments

I must give special mention to my friends and colleagues at the John B. Amos Cancer Center in Columbus, Georgia. You are all very special, and I will always cherish the time I spent with you. Your work truly is God's work, and no one does it better.

Special thanks go to my friends at the University of Miami and the Sylvester Comprehensive Cancer Center for your many years of encouragement and support. I couldn't have survived without your help.

My family provides the motivation for everything I do. Thank you for always being there when I need you and for not laughing when I told you I was writing a book.

To Tom, my true north…may we someday meet for that Cheeseburger in Paradise.

And last but not least, I thank my parents who were with me for far too brief a time but managed to provide the best role models a person could ever ask for.

Chapter One

For better or for worse, today's events would change the world of healthcare forever. This was the point of no return, and Karen Jorgensen struggled with that thought as she lay awake in her bed during the early hours of that historic morning. Although Karen could see that the sky was still pitch dark, she found herself much too excited to sleep. She needed to get up and get started. Throwing off the covers, she grabbed her robe and slippers and jogged to the kitchen. Once there, she perked a pot of her usual dark roast coffee and took a steaming mug out onto the balcony. She sipped the strong brew, watching with delight as the first lavender rays of sunlight broke from the churning sea. Even after living here for almost two years, Karen was still in love with Bermuda. The constant rhythmic sound of the surf hitting the rocks surpassed any symphony she had ever heard. It lulled her to sleep at night and awakened her gently every morning. But there was no gentle awakening this morning. Karen was wide awake long before dawn. This was the day she had looked forward to for the past ten years. This was opening day for Sans Docteur Hospital, the first hospital in the world that would function entirely without medical doctors.

Karen's thoughts drifted back to the day, ten years ago, when the initial idea for Sans Docteur Hospital had been born. Ten years... it seemed like an eternity. She had been working as chief operating officer at a prestigious medical center in the east at the time. The day had been particularly difficult since the board of directors meeting that morning had not gone well. A senior physician had been terminated and many of the old-guard board members were irate. They were especially loud and insulting as they demanded an explanation.

Karen knew that the chief of staff, Dr. Mark Woodens, had only half-heartedly supported the decision to terminate the offending physician, and the big smirk on his face demonstrated his pleasure with the board's hostile reaction.

"Physicians have a right to act any way we want," Dr. Woodens told the board. "We earned our way to the top of the medial hierarchy with our blood, sweat, and tears. Our days are long, and our jobs are extremely stressful. If we need to let off some steam by venting on a nurse or two, so be it. *Besides, most of the nursing staff deserve abuse*. They are always questioning and challenging doctors' orders. *Who do they think they are anyway?* Dr. Arness went a little over the edge by actually striking a nurse, but I can understand that. I've had days when I would have liked to smack one of them myself. When I started out in medicine, the nurses knew their place. They called me 'sir' and stood when I entered the nurses' station. They followed orders without question. If I said it, they did it. And if I needed someone to take my anger out on, the nurses were always available. They knew how to take a little abuse back then. Hell, they expected it."

John Robbins's booming baritone interrupted Dr. Woodens' tirade. "Thank you, Mark. I know you could go on all day, but we need to get back to the meeting." John was the hospital CEO and always spoke and dressed as though he were the leading man in some Broadway show. For emphasis, he waited until he had everyone's undivided attention before he continued. After carefully adjusting the sleeves of his Armani suit, he began his address. "I regret being forced into taking such a strong position," John stated. "I believe that a little slap on the hand would have sufficed. However, the nurses' union had other ideas. They were out for blood, and we had no choice but to terminate Dr. Arness if we wanted to avert a strike. The entire nursing staff would have walked on this one, and most of the others would have gone with them. It would have created a public relations nightmare if the union sharks had contacted their buddies in the press. You know how much they hate us. On the brighter side, legal has assured me that we are on safe ground. Dr. Arness has no defense and certainly no cause for legal action against us. I suggest that we let this unfortunate incident die a natural death and get on to more important issues."

The board members were not happy, but there was nothing more to be said. The sacrifice had been made and could not be retracted. Dr. Arness was collateral damage, and everyone knew it. The board members continued to shake their heads and mumble comments that were best left unsaid, but they reluctantly gave John their vote of support and allowed him to get on with the remainder of the meeting.

As Karen observed the proceedings and listened to the comments, she felt a strong wave of nausea wash over her. Didn't anyone really care? Was it actually okay for a nurse to be struck by a physician? Did a double standard really exist? The answer was obvious as she watched the board members relish their lunch. The assault seemed to be forgotten as they joked and gossiped with the physicians sitting near them. She had to bite her tongue when she overheard one of the senior physicians telling one of his favorite "dumb nurse" jokes about a nurse waking his patient to administer a sleeping pill. The physician actually looked directly at her as he recounted his joke, as though challenging her to say something. Karen clenched her hands into tight fists under the table as she fought to maintain her composure and continue her conversation with one of the more supportive board members. She forced herself to smile even as she admitted to herself that the profession of nursing still had a long, long way to go before it would be given any true measure of respect.

Sans Docteur Hospital

These thoughts haunted Karen through the rest of the meeting. She was tempted to tell the board and the medical leadership exactly what she thought of them when the board chairman announced that it was time for her presentation. Instead, feeling like a coward, Karen gave her usual updates on hospital operations and took her seat to a smattering of applause. Fortunately, there were still a few board members who were always attentive and supportive to Karen and to the nursing service. Unfortunately, they were far outnumbered by the others.

After leaving the meeting, Karen stopped by the office of the chief nursing officer, Barbara Geraci. Barbara stormed around her office, slamming doors and spouting Italian curses under her breath. Karen was not surprised by this in the least bit since Barbara had been very intimately involved in the investigation leading to Dr. Arness's termination. Unlike Karen, Barbara had not stayed at the board meeting to give her usual nursing status report. Instead, pretending that her cell phone had vibrated, she had left the meeting with her phone to her ear, letting the door slam loudly as she made her exit.

"Blast them all!" Barbara said. "They are all animals. The only thing they care about is the almighty bottom line. They would let the doctors take human sacrifices if it meant an increase in the patient census and the gross margins. They don't care about the staff, and they certainly don't care about the patients. Imagine the quality of patient care we could deliver if we didn't have to spend millions on physicians' salaries."

Imagine a hospital without doctors! What would that be like? Was it possible? Karen answered her own question. It was definitely possible. Over the past years, the physicians did less and less of the actual patient care. They delegated almost all of the physical tasks to the nurse practitioners and the nurse specialists. Even the interns and residents had stopped performing actual patient care functions. Karen knew for a fact that nurses could perform all of the patient care and that the nurse practitioners (NPs) could actually perform all of the medical functions that had previously been the exclusive domain of the doctors. New technology was rapidly making physicians the redundant factor. Sophisticated computers directed robotic hands in surgery while the surgeons sat at the consoles, pretending to perform the operations. Other computers directed the mixture of gasses and medications that kept the patients unconscious and comfortable. In the ICU there were sophisticated computer programs that predicted which patients were most likely to die and which could safely be transferred out of the unit and back to the wards.

Yes, she thought, *a hospital without physicians was physically possible, but was it politically possible?* The American Medical Association (AMA) would never allow it. Its members made an extremely powerful coalition. They could make or break any election or politician. No government official or agency would ever go against them and survive. Or would they?

Chapter Two

The ringing telephone snapped Karen back to the present. She hurried inside to answer the phone, dumping her empty cup into the dishwasher on the way. Her sister, Diane, was calling to wish her well with today's opening. Diane, a nurse herself, had not always been in favor of Sans Docteur Hospital. She originally thought that it was the impossible dream and was not shy about telling Karen that she was a fool. However, Karen had recently noted a softening in Diane's attitude but hesitated to comment. She secretly hoped that Diane would one day come and work for her at "the Sans," as the staff loving referred to Sans Docteur Hospital, and she did not want to do or say anything that could hurt her chances.

"I'm just calling to wish you luck and give you some sisterly advice. Take it easy today, and tread very lightly. Don't be too aggressive," said Diane. "You need to keep the press and the Bermuda officials on your side. You can't afford to alienate them. You already have enough enemies praying for you to fail."

"When was I ever too aggressive?" Karen said, laughing.

"When weren't you?" was Diane's instant retort.

"Enough of this bantering. I need to get off to the opening. Watch me on TV, and I'll call you later for your critique."

Karen promised to be on her best behavior as she hung up the phone and ran quickly into the shower, shedding her silk pajamas on the way. Still deep in thought, she quickly brushed her long brown hair. She always kept it neat but casual, and it suited her. She thought lavish makeup and flashy clothes were totally unnecessary. The faint freckles that spread across her nose and cheeks gave her the young, carefree look of youth. Her build was thin and athletic but with all of the feminine curves that made men's heads turn to watch as she passed them by.

Noticing the time, Karen hurriedly dressed in her new Donna Karan suit and jumped into her pearl-white Mercedes convertible. *There is no time to put the top down today*, she thought as she started the powerful engine. It wouldn't do to arrive at the opening looking windblown and sweaty. Gregory would certainly not approve. He thought that women should always be composed and proper. Aside from her financial backers, Gregory was the most important person to influence the successful opening of Sans Docteur Hospital today. As the handsome and charming Honorable Premier of Bermuda, Gregory Andrews III's public endorsement was critical to acceptance of Sans Docteur by both the officials and citizens of Bermuda. The Cabinet and the Ministry of Health would not have given Karen a second thought if not for Gregory's intervention.

Back when Karen had initially pitched the idea for the Sans, Gregory had surprised everyone by putting aside his personal skepticism and going on record as a key supporter. Of course, Karen was sure that this was due in a large part to the generous donations Gregory had received from Marcus MacGregor, the senior partner in WorldHealth, Inc., the corporation that owned the Sans. Marcus was a well-known billionaire who had made his fortune in foreign real estate development. An expert in doing business in foreign cultures, he knew well that bribes were perfectly acceptable in most countries. In fact, bribes were expected and very few deals would have been struck without these bonuses. For sure, the Sans would have remained just a dream if it were not for the several million dollars in bribe money that had been quietly offered and accepted by a few key Bermuda officials. Marcus had assured Karen that he considered this just the normal cost of doing business and that he had found ways to charge the expense back to his other businesses. He boasted that it would take a large team of very bright auditors several months of painstaking work to discover any of these bogus entries. He said that he felt perfectly safe and comfortable with the proceedings.

Marcus had a personal reason for wanting to make the Sans a success. Ten years earlier, his wife, Carla, had been diagnosed with breast cancer. Carla had been just barely fifty at the time of her diagnosis, and both she and Marcus were confident that she would beat the cancer. Marcus had her treated at one of the best cancer centers in the United States. He had personally accompanied her on all visits and ensured that she would get the best of care by donating several million dollars to the cancer center in his wife's name. Despite being assured that Carla would receive top-notch care, Marcus was profoundly disappointed when Carla's care was botched badly right from the beginning. Her initial biopsy specimen was lost on the way to the laboratory. She experienced a serious reaction to the anesthesia during her mastectomy operation and almost died right there on the table. If it were not for a diligent student nurse anesthetist, Carla's distress would have gone unnoticed and untreated. The student nurse had alerted the anesthesiologist who had been busy texting his girlfriend instead of monitoring the patient. Her quick intervention allowed the reaction to be treated before it became fatal.

Chemotherapy had also turned into a nightmare for Carla, who had been constantly fatigued and nauseated during the treatments. Within months of her diagnosis, Carla had lost forty pounds and looked twenty years older. Her beautiful, blonde, curly hair had fallen out and her peaches-and-cream complexion had taken on a dry, gray appearance so common in AIDS and cancer patients. She couldn't even bear to look in the mirror at the end, and Marcus, ever the caring husband, had all mirrors removed or covered to spare her any further pain.

The physicians went through the motions of trying to cure her, but their behavior was cold and uncaring. They simply told Marcus that medicine is an art, and not a science. Sometimes things do not turn out as planned. Some patients failed despite the physicians' best efforts and treatments. Marcus understood their meaning here. The patients failed, not the physicians. The physicians had actually made it seem that it was Carla's fault that she was dying and not theirs.

Carla lost her sight and her mind when the cancer spread to her brain. Despite weeks of radiation therapy, she never really recovered her memory or her personality. By the time Carla died, Marcus was totally disillusioned with the practice of medicine and disgusted with physicians. He made a promise to Carla as he stood looking down at her grave. He would avenge her death and make those doctors pay for what they had done. It would be his personal crusade.

A few years later, Marcus read about Karen's plan for a hospital without doctors and knew instantly that this was his chance to make a difference and even the score with the medical profession. He couldn't help Carla, but he could ensure that hundreds of other sick people would receive the care that Carla had been denied. Calling Karen, he told her to start looking for a location. The Sans would have all the money necessary to make it the best healthcare facility in the world. Within months, he had secured three additional investors and formed the

WorldHealth Corporation, a for-profit healthcare firm that would provide total financing for the Sans. Karen's wish was answered. Sans Docteur Hospital would be a reality.

Chapter Three

Arriving at the Sans just a few hours before the opening ceremonies, Karen found chaos. Her executive staff members were running around in a panic, trying in vain to gain control of the situation. As always, Karen's composed presence calmed them. Things immediately started to fall into place and, within minutes, order was restored as if by magic.

Karen's assistant, Maureen, was obviously impressed and relieved. "I don't know how you do it," Maureen declared. "Five minutes ago I was ready to head for the hills, and now I'm ready to take on the world. What is it about you that gives everyone such confidence? I need to bottle it and feed it to the staff when you are not around."

Karen laughed out loud and hugged Maureen warmly. "It's all in your head," she said jokingly. "You only think you need me. You could do my job all by yourself by now. But don't try yet," she added quickly.

"I'm not quite ready for retirement. I think I'm going to like this job, and I intend to keep it for a long, long time."

Before Maureen could object, Gregory Andrews III arrived, demanding Karen's undivided attention as always. "Are we ready?" asked Gregory.

Karen smiled and winked conspiratorially at Maureen. She felt more than saw Gregory's impatience and snapped to attention. "Of course," she replied taking his arm and smiling up at him. "We were just waiting for you, Gregory. Now that you're here, we can get started."

With that, Karen and Gregory took their place on the stage along with Marcus and the three other owners of World Health Corporation. Looking out at the audience, Karen was impressed. Everyone who was anyone in Bermuda government and society was there. But more impressive was the presence of the US press corps and a multitude of US officials. Vice President Melanie Gorden was the most prestigious, but she was certainly not alone. Karen recognized executives from America's top medical organizations and the AMA sitting in the front row. It was a sea of blue suits and red ties as far as the eye could see.

Fighting back a sudden wave of nausea, Karen rose to walk to the podium. It was only a few feet but it felt like miles. Looking out at the audience, she nervously adjusted the microphone. Panic was starting to set in as Vice President Gorden caught Karen's eye and smiled her encouragement. She discreetly signaled a double thumbs-up, and Karen instantly relaxed as she smiled back and started her speech. After welcoming everyone, she went on to thank them for being there on the most important day in healthcare history. Her speech took over thirty minutes, but to Karen it seemed like just seconds had elapsed as she delivered her final comments. There were cheers and thunderous applause as she concluded and then introduced Gregory Andrews III.

Karen tried to concentrate on the remaining speeches, but it was impossible. She was just too excited to pay much attention to the words. The next hour went by in a blur. Before she knew it she was thanking everyone for coming and inviting them to enjoy appetizers and cocktails and to join her for a VIP tour of the Sans.

Karen stood in the reception line as hundreds of famous and affluent people stopped to congratulate her and wish her well. Forcing herself to concentrate, she addressed each by name. She prided herself on her ability to correctly place names with faces and seldom faltered. By the time Barbara and her husband, John, brought up the rear of the line, Karen was exhausted. Linking arms, they steered her out to the patio and the bar. John handed her a glass of champagne and raised his glass in a toast.

"Here's to the best hospital in the world and the best boss ever," he said into the microphone, and Barbara raised her glass in agreement. As if on cue, the entire staff of the Sans stood and repeated his sentiment as they raised their glasses in salute. The applause from the officials and other visitors was deafening. Karen blushed as she raised her glass and saluted them back.

A chill ran down her spine as she watched the three men scowling at her from the back of the room. They slammed their glasses onto the nearest table. Pushing their way rudely through the crowd, they managed to jostle several dignitaries as they hurried to the exit door. She couldn't help but notice the numerous glares and mumbled complaints that followed their hasty exit.

"To the best staff in the world," Karen replied as John pushed the microphone into her hand. "I wouldn't be here today if it weren't for your hard work and dedication. Now, everyone fill your glasses, and let me show you the most beautiful oncology hospital ever built!"

Karen headed for the inpatient pavilion as fifty people followed close behind. She glowed as she led them through the beautiful patient rooms and pointed out the incredible views from every room.

Everyone laughed when the CBS news anchor, John Simmons, called out, "Karen, can I reserve a room here? I know I'm not sick, but the views are so much better than the ones at my hotel."

"I don't think CBS would cover the daily room rate, John," Karen quipped back. "It's a little higher than your typical hotel bill."

Even the hardcore critics had trouble denying that they were impressed by the massive size and the abundance of computerized equipment in the state-of-the-art surgical suites. Karen paused in the largest suite to point out the computer-driven robots. She explained how the robots performed the surgery as the nurses and the nurse anesthetists assisted and that the robots had a 100-percent accuracy rate—something that no surgeon, no matter how competent, could ever claim. Human beings are fallible, and they make mistakes. But, computers can and do perform at top capacity even in the last surgery of a twenty-four-hour day. Computers don't get tired, and their hands don't shake. They never have personal problems to think about during surgery. They always gave their full attention to the job at hand and, thus, are always successful.

By the time the tour ended back in the lobby, everyone was in agreement that the Sans was as beautiful as any five-star luxury resort and much more impressive than any hospital they had ever seen. However, the beauty of the surroundings and the presence of state-of-the-art equipment did not fully dispel the worries about the lack of medical doctors. The Sans' staff had a long way to go before they could convince anyone that a hospital could function completely without doctors.

Chapter Four

The next morning arrived all too quickly for Karen. Gone were the beautiful sunny skies of the previous day. Rain clouds, lightning, and frequent explosions of deafening thunder had replaced them. Karen hoped that this was not an omen of things to come as feelings of dread swept over her.

Now that the construction and the opening ceremonies were done, it was time to open the facility and begin admitting patients. This was the real moment of truth. *Would patients actually come to the Sans? Would they accept medical care without physicians? Could they possibly understand?* Saying a silent prayer, Karen walked into the lobby of the Sans. She stopped on the way to her office to watch the security guard unlock the front door for the first time. Certainly, anyone wanting to receive cancer care in beautiful surroundings would appreciate the Sans. It was perfect. Perched on a point just west of Fort St. Catherine, it overlooked crashing blue waves and had the most breathtaking views of any hospital in the world. No one could ask for a better site. They had been so lucky to have purchased the land just before a developer snatched up all of the surrounding land for a new golf course.

The Sans overlooked Tobacco Bay and one of the most beautiful golf courses in the world. The location, which was just minutes east of Bermuda International Airport, was ideal. And the facility surpassed the site. It was fashioned after classic Hawaiian architecture. During the day, the lobby doors pushed back to allow an eighty-foot-wide opening. Powerful air blowers kept the warm air out and the cool air in. The huge plantation fans were not really necessary, but they did add to the ambiance. Everything here emulated a five-star hotel. Even the patients looked more like guests than patients. They were given loose-flowing outfits that were more suited to an expensive spa than a hospital. No embarrassing, hospital-style patient gowns were allowed here. Karen and the staff firmly believed that looking good went hand-in-hand with feeling good, and they made sure that their patients looked and felt as good as possible.

Everything at the Sans was geared to improving the patients' emotional, physical, and mental state during the most vulnerable periods of the patients' lives. Even the sickest of cancer patients would have trouble maintaining a depression at the Sans. It was just too nice, too uplifting.

Karen had initially won over the Bermuda officials with her insistence on sustainable "green design," which reduces the consumption of non-renewable resources, manages waste, and creates a healthy productive environment. She had attracted the best clinical staff by her staff-sparing design which eliminated wasted movement and reduced staff fatigue, which has a direct correlation with medical errors. Utilizing the architects best known for designing safe, efficient hospitals in the States, Karen had challenged them to design an even safer, more efficient hospital, and they had not let her down. The Sans was the most cutting-edge, state-of-the-art healthcare facility ever built. No other hospital in the world could compare with the Sans. The only thing missing was the physician component, and Karen thought that was a plus.

Chapter Five

The first patient admitted to the Sans was the wife of the infamous Senator Brian Charles. Cynthia Charles had been diagnosed with breast cancer eighteen months ago. Upon hearing the diagnosis, the senator had immediately flown his wife up north for a second opinion at one of the best cancer centers in the States. The cancer diagnosis was confirmed, and she had immediately undergone a unilateral radical mastectomy and started on an aggressive course of chemotherapy and radiation therapy. It was a treatment plan obviously designed to either kill or cure, and Cynthia was not sure which she had experienced. Some days she felt so bad that the kill option actually looked good to her. On the worst days, she simply stayed in bed and prayed for the end. Her physician and his staff did not even seem to notice. They visited her every day and did their poking and prodding. They asked the rote questions. "How are we today? Are we feeling better?" They never waited for an answer. They looked at the entries on her chart and whispered to each other before leaving the room without a backward glance. Cynthia wished that just once they would really look at her, really listen to her. But that never happened.

She really couldn't complain. They treated her as well as anyone else and better than most since she was a VIP. The staff at the center was professional but remote. They made her feel like just another number. No one seemed to care about her as a person. She was just the patient in room 592, another statistic to the physicians and staff and another chance to claim success for the medical community.

Cynthia had endured the treatments silently. She went through the radical mastectomy and the chemo and radiation therapy without complaint. Afterward she was told that she was cured. *Cured.* What a wonderful word! Too bad it wasn't true.

A month ago, she had returned to her oncologist for a routine checkup, fully expecting a clean bill of health. After submitting to the routine blood work and the usual scans, she met with her oncologist, Dr. Sloat. His steely gray eyes looked right through people, never actually focusing on any one person. When Dr. Sloat refused to make even his special version of eye contact today, Cynthia began to worry. Brian, her husband, was the first to break the silence. "What's wrong, Sloat?" he asked.

"I'm afraid the news is not good," Sloat said. "The cancer is back, and it's now in the other breast.

She should have had the bi-lateral mastectomy like I recommended."

Cynthia felt like she had been slapped. "Don't talk about me like I'm not here!" she screamed. "You most certainly did not recommend a double mastectomy. You simply said that it was an option. If you had told me that it was necessary, I would have had it. Don't try to change your story now."

Dr. Sloat had been characteristically condescending. He smiled sympathetically at Brian, and Brian responded in kind, ignoring Cynthia as though she were invisible. "What do we do now, Sloat?"

Sloat recommended another surgery to be followed by more radiation. Brian stated that it should be done the following week. Cynthia decided that it should not. She had another plan in mind. She had recently read about the Sans in an article in the local newspaper. The idea of a hospital with no medical doctors had intrigued her. According to the article, professional advanced practice nurses and nursing staff would provide all the care. Computers would decide the best course of treatment and would guide the robots that would perform any necessary surgery. Cynthia was sick of smug, condescending doctors who refused to answer her questions and patted her on the head when she had concerns. If she needed more treatment, she would have it at the Sans. Brian would not be happy, but he would have no choice. This time she would have her way. This was her disease and her life she would make this decision with or without Brian's consent. She was going to the Sans, and that was that.

Now that she was finally at the Sans, Cynthia was even more certain that she had been right to leave the States and come here. Just the way the staff had greeted her on her arrival had made her feel better. The fact that each and every one of them made eye contact and sat down to speak with her whenever they came into her room made her feel important. They always gave her the impression that they had all the time in the world just for her. She knew they must have other patients to attend to, but they never seemed rushed or impatient. This was a totally new experience and one that she could definitely get used to. She was going to like the Sans. No doubt about it.

On the other hand, Brian was furious. He told Cynthia that he couldn't believe that she had arrived at this decision without his consent and totally against his wishes. He insisted that she had made him look foolish in front of Dr. Sloat and his staff, acting as though their opinions were more important than Cynthia's life. Actually, the more Brian objected, the more Cynthia believed in her choice. For the first time in her married life she had started to doubt Brian's sincerity and wondered if he really wanted her to get well. Maybe he would rather that she die quickly and free him to find some twenty-year-old child like so many of his cronies had done. She didn't want to believe that about her husband, but she couldn't help but wonder.

Chapter Six

The rest of Karen's day had gone by in a blur. In all, twenty-three patients were admitted and over a hundred outpatients were seen in the ambulatory clinics. This was astonishing and far better than Karen had hoped for. She and the rest of the senior staff met in the boardroom at the end of the day. They were all exhausted but happy as they congratulated each other and fell into their seats with relief. Most of them had been on their feet for the past twelve hours.

As she took her seat at the head of the table, Karen looked around the room and smiled at everyone. "Thank you all," she said. "This day couldn't have been a success without you. You each played an essential part in getting us here. The Sans is truly a team effort, and you are a great team! I couldn't have hoped for a better first day. Now, let's all get some rest. This is going to be a killer week, and I need you all in good shape. I know that you are happy, but please hold the celebrations until the weekend. Don't forget. I expect all of you at my open house Saturday night. I have tons of food and the booze is going to flow like water. We are all going to party till the sun comes up! Now, get out of here!"

Karen did not follow her own advice. She immediately went back to her office and began opening her e-mails and voicemails. There were at least twenty phone calls and over one hundred e-mails to be answered. After pouring herself a cup of coffee, she began the onerous task of answering each one.

The remainder of the week flew by without incident. Patients came by the dozens and Karen was both pleased and amazed. The in-patient census list read like societies' Who's Who column. Almost every patient was a notable American. Every one of them was demanding and exacting. And, to a person, everyone was pleased with the care at the Sans. The treatment team rounded on the patients at least twice a day taking time to actually speak with each patient and with any family members present. They answered all questions and put all concerns to rest. No request was denied if it could be granted. No matter how big or how small the issue, the staff responded. The word *no* was never heard. So far, no patient had complained about the lack of physicians, and Karen wondered how long luck would hold. How long would it be before someone with a bad outcome would try to blame the lack of physician supervision for the inevitable result?

Karen feared that her luck had run out when Mrs. Roberts, wife of the late president, called Karen's office, asking that Karen visit her. Karen said a silent prayer and set out for Mrs. Roberts's room. Taking a deep breath, she pushed open the door to room 315. Mrs. Roberts appeared to be sleeping restlessly. She was tossing side to side and talking in her sleep. Karen was tempted to make a quick exit, but she resisted. There was something in Mrs. Roberts's face that held her attention. The distress on the older woman's face was evident. Mrs. Roberts was obviously in pain, and there was no way Karen could just walk out and leave her like that. She called Mrs. Roberts's name, but the patient did not respond. Karen then put her hand on the frail woman's shoulder and shook her gently. She saw the patient's eyes flutter and then open and attempt to focus. Karen remained silent with her hand on the patient's shoulder until she felt the patient relax.

Mrs. Roberts looked up at Karen and tried to smile. "You must be Mrs. Jorgensen," she said hoarsely.

"Please, call me Karen," Karen replied without even thinking. "I understand that you have been asking to speak with me. Is there a problem that I can help you with?"

Mrs. Roberts smiled back at Karen as she looked around the pleasant hospital room. "No, child," she replied. "I didn't call you to complain. Just the opposite. I called you to tell you how much I like it here. I have been in the best cancer centers in the United States. But none of them were anything like Sans Docteur. This is the best hospital I have ever been in. The staff not only makes you feel at home, but they actually make you feel like they really care about you. They actually listen to me and respond to my requests. It's the damndest thing

I've ever seen. I really believe that they care—about me, about my feelings. How do you do that? How do you actually get them to care?"

Karen looked down at Mrs. Roberts and sighed. She knew the answer, but she was reluctant to share it. She wasn't sure that the patient would believe her. "Our clinical staff was hand-picked. Each and every one of them went through rigorous psychological testing. Only those with extremely high scores in critical thinking and empathy were selected to work at Sans Docteur. We don't just accept anyone. Each one of our staff members is special. And, their jobs depend on making each and every patient feel special. We wouldn't be here if it weren't for the patients and their needs, and we acknowledge that personally and professionally. I'm very glad to hear that they my staff have made you comfortable."

Mrs. Roberts appeared to study Karen for a long time. Finally, she said, "Call me Carolynn. Mrs. Roberts is my mother-in-law, and I have never been too fond of her. She is a very rich, pompous woman. She never accepted me as her darling son's wife. He could have done a lot better according to her. A factory worker's daughter was not her idea of an acceptable wife for her son. Unfortunately, after several years, she convinced him of that as well, and it was downhill from then on. I would probably have been left penniless if she had had her way. But God had other intentions. John died in a car accident before she could get him to divorce me. Now, I have all of his money and his possessions, and Mrs. Roberts has to come to me for her support, which really galls her. But, she's learned to swallow her pride and beg very well. She'd rather deal with me than do without. To her, there's nothing worse than being destitute," Carolynn blurted out, without stopping for a breath. Karen had no idea why Mrs. Roberts had just divulged the personal details of her entire life to a virtual stranger. She knew from the little that had been written in the tabloids that the woman was normally very private about her life.

Karen smiled at Carolynn knowingly. "I can think of many things that are worse than being poor. Your mother-in-law should be eternally grateful if that's the worst thing she can think of. Someday she will experience the worse things first hand. In the meantime, she is lucky to have a daughter-in-law like you who is willing to take care of her. Most people in your situation would delight in watching her suffer."

Carolynn began to cry softly. "I've seen enough suffering. I wouldn't wish that on anyone, not even my mother-in-law. God will deal with her in his own time. He has his way of making us all humble in the end. Meanwhile, I have all I can do to deal with my own problems. I can handle all of it except for the pain. When the pain gets really bad, I just wish I could end it. Take a few too many pills and never wake up. But, since I have been here at the Sans, the pain has lessened significantly. It's almost non-existent now. The pain block that the nurse anesthetist, Sharon, gave me did the trick. In fact, sometimes I actually forget about the cancer and pretend that I'm at a fancy health spa, spending John's money. That always makes me feel better. And it's not hard to do in these beautiful surroundings. The view out my window is breathtaking! I love just sitting here, looking at it."

Taking Carolynn's hand gently, Karen thanked her for the kind words, wished her well, and left promising to stop back soon. Karen knew that was a promise that she would gladly keep. She actually looked forward to meeting with the patients at the Sans. This was a new experience and one that she would enjoy getting used to. In all of her other hospitals, she had dreaded speaking with patients and families. They always wanted to complain about something. Most of the time, they were angry with the doctors but wouldn't dare voice those complaints. Instead, they would complain about the staff. Any little thing would do. Even a pill that was ten minutes late could bring an angry outburst. The patients and the families needed an outlet for their frustration and their anger, and the nursing staff provided that outlet. The staff bore the punishment for of all of the physicians' transgressions. After all, how could a patient make his physician angry? Who knew what would happen to the medical care if the physicians were angry? Would the visits get later and later? Would they be shorter and shorter? Worse yet, would the physician stop visiting altogether and send some resident instead? These were all valid worries and in her time Karen had seen examples of all of them. Physicians could be crass and vindictive when angered. Some even seemed to enjoy abusing patients. Fortunately, these were a very small percentage of the overall physician population. Most physicians had seemed to just withdraw. They always seemed to find other more important duties that would take them far away from the bedside and direct patient care. In the end, they had finally managed to delegate all patient care to the NPs and nurses, leaving the door wide open for the Sans to become a reality.

Chapter Seven

Karen's private line was ringing when she opened the door to her office. Looking down at the caller ID, she noted with delight that it was her friend, Ted Richards. Karen and Ted had been inseparable back in graduate school, and their friendship had endured for over a decade despite Robert's disapproval. Smiling, Karen picked up the phone and immediately heard Ted's voice.

"Well, it's about time! I thought you might have disappeared into the Triangle. It's been much too long since I've heard from you. Actually, I did see you on TV the other night so I knew you must be alive. I'm sorry that I missed the opening. It looked like a huge success, judging from the press coverage. I've not seen that many stuffy dignitaries in one placed since the inauguration! What did you do? Bribe someone?"

"Very funny," Karen replied. "It would have been very nice if my best friend could have found time in his busy schedule to come and lend some moral support. This is all a little overwhelming, you know. What is it that's keeping you so busy anyway?"

Karen knew the answer. Ted was a very busy primary care physician. One of the few doctors left who still saw patients himself, he was even known to make house calls out in the Seattle suburb where he lived. Ted loved practicing medicine, and he loved his patients. Ever since his wife had left him and took their daughter with her, Ted had totally devoted himself to his practice. Karen worried about him and had, on more than one occasion, tried to convince him to come over to Bermuda for a long and well-deserved vacation.

"Actually," Ted replied, "I was calling to tell you that I found someone to cover for me for the next few weeks, and I thought that I would come over there and check you out. I've been worried about you. I can only imagine the hours you put in. I know how important this is to you, but you shouldn't overdo it. Even God rested on the seventh day," Ted teased. "So how about it? Can I crash with you for a while? Will you take a little time off and show me around your island?"

Karen couldn't have been more delighted, but at the same time, she was concerned. Ted never took time off, and he never turned his patients over to anyone else. What was going on here?

"I guess I could put up with you for a while," she said. "Robert is in Germany on business, and he probably won't be back for at least a week or two. He also missed my opening. You two are definitely two of a kind! You can come and stay with me in the villa, and we can scandalize the town and give the gossip moguls something to talk about. How soon can you get here? I'm having a big party Saturday night, and you could help me host it."

"I can take the early morning flight from New York and be there by noon. I'll grab a ride out to the villa so don't worry about picking me up. You've got a lot to do to get ready for your bash, and I don't want to take you away. Well, I gotta run. My next patient just arrived, and you know how I am about keeping patients waiting. See you Saturday."

The phone went dead. That was typical Ted. He never waited for an answer or a good-bye. Not one to waste time, he said what he had to say and that was that. As she hung up the phone, Karen realized how much she had missed Ted. Actually, she missed him more than she was missing her husband, Robert. She had been relieved when Robert had told her about his trip to Germany. Even though it had meant that he would miss her opening, she had not been the least bit upset. Robert was a high-maintenance type of person. He was always in need of her time and her attention. It was easier to concentrate on the details for the opening in his absence. Besides, he had to be the center of attention. He would not have enjoyed seeing the spotlight on Karen.

It had always been this way. Even back before they were married, Robert had been demanding. She had to admit that he was not the one who had changed. Truth be told, Robert had not changed one bit. Maybe that was the key to their problem. In ten years of marriage, shouldn't both partners grow and mature? Shouldn't they each be at least a little different? Certainly, Karen was different. She now knew what she wanted and it wasn't to play mother to Robert. No, Robert would finally have to learn to stand on his own and feed his own ego. At least that was what she told herself when he was away.

Invariably, that was not the way it was when Robert was home. The minute he returned from a trip, Karen would revert back to being the little woman. She would cook and do his laundry and entertain his friends. Life revolved around Robert. No doubt about it. Robert was the master in this marriage.

But, each time he went away, Karen became stronger in her resolve. One day soon things would change. It was inevitable. Karen was a competent, take-charge person in her public life, and she needed to be the same in her personal life as well. A drastic change was coming.

Chapter Eight

Saturday arrived and with it came a whirlwind of activity. Karen was up at daybreak, and by the time the coffee was brewed, she had already checked off over half the items on her to-do list. Within an hour, the ovens were giving off wonderful aromas, and pots were steaming on every burner of the commercial-grade stove in her spacious kitchen.

Karen had already showered and dressed in tailored jeans and a white T-shirt by the time Ted arrived. As always, he greeted her with the warm bear hug that never failed to make Karen feel safe and secure. Ted lifted her off her feet, swung her around, and then put her down and stepped back to look at her.

Karen regained her footing and smiled up at him. "You know I'm getting too old for that. One of these days you are going to break me clean in half," she joked.

"Never happen," said Ted. "You just get tougher with age. Although, you do look a little tired. Don't you believe in sleeping anymore?"

"We'll sleep in tomorrow after the party. We have too much to do now. Put your bags up in the guestroom to the right of the stairs. Grab yourself a cup of coffee, and start rearranging the furniture. We need to clear space for the dance floor and the buffet tables. Now get going." She good-naturedly gave Ted a shove, and he took off up the steps, carrying his luggage as though it was as light as a feather.

With Ted's help, Karen flew through the chores in no time. They even found time to take a short walk on the beach and enjoy a glass of wine while watching the sunset before the party. It was a beautiful sunset, and Karen couldn't remember when she had enjoyed one more. She felt content and relaxed and was more than a little surprised to find that she was looking forward to the evening's activities. Normally, she dreaded entertaining, but this was different. This was not one of Robert's stuffy dinner parties. This was a casual open house for the people she cared about the most—her staff at the Sans. They were like family to her, and she would not have had the fortitude to pitch the plans for the Sans without their never-ending encouragement and support. The long hours they worked without complaint proved how much they believed in the Sans. They enjoyed their work, and it showed. Now it was her turn to show them her appreciation in the only way she knew—by opening her home and her heart to them.

Ted took Karen's hand as they strolled along the beach, and he stopped to smile down at her on more than one occasion. Each time Karen looked up into his eyes, her breath would catch, and her heart would skip a beat. She couldn't understand it. This was Ted—Ted, her best friend. Why was he suddenly having this effect on her?

She pulled her hand away and broke into a jog to hide her embarrassment. "Come on, old man. We need to get back before you're too tired to party," she shouted back at him.

He laughed and shook his head before following her. They were both laughing and breathless when they reached the villa. Catching her hand, Ted spun her toward him as they entered the great room. He stared down at her smiling face and Karen feared that he was about to kiss her. Pulling away for the second time, she ran up the stairs to her bedroom and slammed the door. Karen leaned back against the door, feeling weak and confused. Had Ted been about to kiss her, or had she just misinterpreted his intention? She blushed as she thought back on it. No, this was crazy. It was just her imagination and the effects of wine, sunset, and the warm breezes. Ted was her friend. Nothing more. She was a married woman and shouldn't be having these fantasies about anyone other than Robert. She resolved to keep her feelings in check for the remainder of Ted's visit. After all, the last thing she wanted to do was to compromise their long-standing friendship.

The sound of the door slamming brought Ted back to reality. Regaining his composure, he slowly made his way to the guestroom. As he undressed and slipped into the shower, he couldn't stop thinking about Karen. Was she in the shower on the other side of the wall? Was she thinking of him? He hoped so. He was in love with her, and he prayed that she felt the same about him. That is what he had come to Bermuda to find out. Did she love him, too? Would she end this farce of a marriage to Robert and marry him instead or had he waited too long? He wished that he had realized his feelings for Karen years ago before she had married Robert. But back then he had been married and, although he was not deeply in love with his wife, he was fiercely loyal to her. It was only after his wife had left him and taken their daughter, Mary, that Ted had begun to allow himself to think of Karen as anything more than a friend. It had come to him during one of the endless hours of therapy that he had endured after the crash of his marriage. His psychologist had challenged him to think of the positive things in his life, and his friendship with Karen was the only good thing that he could come up with. The psychologist had looked at him with that "aha" look, and Ted knew immediately what he must do. He could waste no more of his life. He would go to Karen and ask her to leave Robert and spend her life with him.

Now that he was here in Bermuda with Karen, Ted was surer than ever that he loved her. But, at the same time, he was rapidly losing his nerve. Looking at all she had here with Robert, he experienced more than one second thought. Why would Karen want to give up all that Robert had given her to marry someone like Ted? What could he offer her? His small private practice certainly did not afford him anywhere near the wealth that Robert and his family had acquired. No, there was no way that he could compete with this. He made up his mind to keep his feelings to himself and just enjoy the remainder of his visit with his friend. Before he could change his mind, he threw on his clothes and hurried downstairs to fix himself a stiff drink.

As Karen changed into her party clothes, the bell rang. She heard Ted laughing and talking to the caterer. By the time she made her grand entrance down the front stairwell, everything was ready. All of the decorations had been placed out on the patio and in the great room, and the tables were straining under the burden of mounds of mouth-watering Caribbean food. Ted had her favorite Hawaiian Island music playing on the stereo and had lit all of the candles and lanterns. A huge fire was crackling in the fireplace. The great room doors were all open onto the patio, and the effect was magical. It all looked surreal in the candlelight. Taking her hand, Ted led Karen in a slow dance out to the patio. Karen couldn't believe how relaxed she felt as she and Ted swayed to the music. The gentle breeze and the rhythmic sound of the waves crashing on the rocks heightened the feeling of relaxation. Karen only hoped that her guests would enjoy tonight's party as much as she was already enjoying it.

Gustavo, the caterer, smiled as he watched Karen and Ted out on the patio. They were so obviously in love. He hurried to finish adding the garnish to the giant seafood platters as the waiters completed the bars and hors d'oeuvres tables. He motioned to them not to disturb the couple on the patio, and they nodded their agreement.

When the music stopped, Gustavo clapped happily. "I envy you two. You are such a beautiful couple. I wish my wife and I were still as romantic as you two."

Ted just laughed, but Karen turned red. "Gustavo, this is not my husband. Robert is away on business. This is my friend, Ted. Dr. Theodore Richards."

Now it was Gustavo's turn to redden. "I am so sorry, Mrs. Jorgenson. I just assumed that this gentleman was your husband since he was here alone in the villa with you. I don't know how to apologize."

Ted laughed again and put his hand out to Gustavo. "It's my fault. I should have introduced myself properly when I answered the door earlier. I am just the poor, old, lonely friend that the Jorgensons take pity on every once in a while and allow to bask in their luxurious surroundings. I am honored that you mistook me for the great Robert Jorgenson. Robert wouldn't be too happy about it, though. I wouldn't mention it to him when you meet him."

Gustavo just shook his head and backed out of the room. Karen agreed. Robert would not be happy about Gustavo's mistake. In fact, he wouldn't be happy about Ted's visit at all. Robert did not understand Karen's affection for Ted. After all, Ted was a physician, and Karen was not supposed to like physicians. As many times as she tried to explain her friendship with Ted, Karen could never get through to Robert. She wasn't sure if it was Robert's controlling nature or just plain jealousy, but Robert did not like Ted one bit. Karen prayed that Robert would not call until later in the week. She was dreading the battle that would surely ensue when he discovered that Ted was in Bermuda. But there was no time for those thoughts now. There would be time enough after the party. And Karen was not going to let anything spoil her fun tonight. She had worked long and hard for this night, and she was going to enjoy it.

Barbara Geraci, Karen's best friend, was the first to arrive. Barbara and her husband, John, came directly to the kitchen to find Karen.

"We came a little early. What can we do to help?" Barbara asked as she hugged Karen.

"Nothing left to do but sample the wine, and we've already started," Karen said. "What will it be: red, white, or blush?"

"We'll have red, and what do you mean by 'we'? Is Robert back already?" Barbara asked, not bothering to mask the dread in her voice.

"No, you can relax. Robert is a few thousand miles away. My friend Ted is here."

Barbara smiled knowingly. "Whew, that's a relief. No offense, but I'm not up to a night with the great Robert Jorgensen. This week has been stressful enough. Now Ted is a different story. Him I like. I always thought that you two would end up together someday."

"Enough of that," Karen said. "You know that Ted and I are only friends. There has never been anything more, and there never will be. And, while we are on the subject, there is nothing wrong with Robert. You just need to give him a chance. He just takes time to warm up to people."

As Barbara mumbled, "Global warming couldn't thaw Robert Jorgenson," Ted appeared. He had obviously overheard part of the conversation since he came bearing two full glasses of the red wine.

"Hello, Barb. How's my favorite chief nurse?" he bellowed, giving her a peck on the cheek as he handed her one of the glasses of red wine. He shook hands warmly with John and handed him the other glass of wine. "Hi, John. How've you been? Or, should I guess? You must have your hands full with these two. They are more than any one man should be expected to manage."

"No complaints. I've got it pretty good. I have the best wife in the world and the best boss in the world. And I'm not just saying that because they are both here. I really mean it. Things have never been better for me. How about you? What are you doing on the other side of the world? How did Karen pry you loose from your practice?"

For a moment a dark look came over Ted's face. It was fleeting, but it did not go unnoticed by any of the three who knew him well. "I'm okay, I guess. I'll fill you in when we have more time," Ted replied mysteriously as Barbara and John exchanged knowing looks above Karen's head. John knew better than to press Ted. They had all been pretty close friends back in North Carolina when they worked together at the medical center.

Guests started to arrive in small groups, and Karen quickly became too busy to give any more thought to Barbara's comments. The night was magical. The music and the lights were mesmerizing, and Gustavo had outdone himself on the food. Overflowing trays of Alaskan salmon, New England lobster, giant shrimp, and sushi-grade tuna seemed to magically replenish themselves. Drinks flowed, and the band played hit after hit as the guests crowded the dance floor. It was a perfect evening, and both Karen and Ted reveled in the feeling of love and acceptance that seemed to radiate from every guest. They appeared to all of the party goers as they had appeared to Gustavo: the perfect couple. Everyone recognized that fact except for the couple themselves.

Ted was the highlight of the evening. He was a true man's man, but he was also warm and considerate of the women—a very unusual combination. At some point during the evening he had found time to joke or share a story with each one of Karen's guests. As Karen and

Ted danced to the last slow song of the evening, there was not a person in the room who did not notice their mutual attraction. They appeared to have found what very few people find in a lifetime—a soul mate.

Chapter Nine

Karen's husband, Robert Jorgenson was a stiff and formal man who lacked the ability to make others feel at home. That was probably because he really never cared how anyone else felt. Karen's staff members were only invited to his parties as window dressings, and they were only allowed when the occasion demanded that Karen's associates be present. Actually, if he were to have his preference, he would never see any of them again. Karen would give up this silly preoccupation with a hospital without doctors and stay at home and take care of him, his household, and his needs. After all, they certainly didn't need the money. His business provided more than enough income, and he had inherited enough family money to allow him to live in the lap of luxury for the rest of his days without ever earning another cent. No, Robert didn't understand why Karen insisted on working. His mother had never worked and neither did his sister-in-law. They were the stereotypical trophy wives, and that was exactly what Robert wanted—a wife who lived to support him and meet his needs. He had no time or patience for trying to meet Karen's needs.

Karen was an embarrassment to Robert, who secretly hoped that the Sans would fail and that Karen would finally give up this obsession. And, it was about time. He was sure that Karen's preoccupation with her work was the reason they were childless. It was not a low sperm count. Karen had probably coerced the doctor into giving them that as an excuse as a way of blaming their failure on him. Robert knew for sure that it wasn't his fault. After all, hadn't he fathered a child with Tina? Tina had only been his mistress for three months when she turned up pregnant. Despite his normal pessimism, Robert immediately knew that the child she was carrying was his. He felt it. And, if he had any doubts, they disappeared when Tina gave birth. His son, William, was the spitting image of Robert and would be the only male who could carry on the Jorgensen family name. But Robert would never openly acknowledge the child as his as long as this sham marriage to Karen existed. It was pure torture to him. He wanted more than anything to end this marriage and make a new life with Tina, but divorce was not an option in his book. People of his social stature simply did not divorce. It was too scandalous. Karen would have to be eliminated if he was ever to live the life he deserved. He prayed that Karen would die, but at the same time, he recognized that prayer was not the answer. He would have to take matters into his own hands at some point but not right now. Now, he was enjoying a long vacation in New Jersey in a home he had purchased for Tina and William. Here he was able to enjoy the life that he had only dreamt of with Karen. Tina was the perfect match for Robert. Her only ambition in life was to care for him and William and make them happy. Robert's every wish was met before he even spoke it. Tina seemed to have an infallible intuition for Robert's needs and was undeniably devoted to satisfying them. Robert knew that she lived for the times when Robert was there at home with her and William. Over and over, she told him that nothing made her happier than pretending that Robert was her husband and William's father. He had no doubt that she believed him wholeheartedly when he promised that one day he would be free to marry her. Then the pretense would be over and the three of them could live openly as a family. Until that day came, he trusted that Tina would continue to do everything within her power to make him happy.

Chapter Ten

After the final guests left, Karen and Ted supervised the clean-up crew and put most of the furniture back into its normal place. It was well past midnight, but the couple appeared to be too keyed up to even think about sleep. Bouncing in from the patio, Ted declared the night a total success. "What a beautiful night. I don't know the last time I enjoyed myself so much. Look at those stars…they're amazing. We can't go to sleep without one more walk on the beach." He shouted to Karen, "Stop cleaning and grab the last open bottle of champagne! We're going for a moonlight walk."

Coming in from the kitchen with the champagne tucked under one arm, Karen took Ted's hand and led him down to the beach in silence. As they settled comfortably on the beach chaise, Karen gratefully took the glass that Ted handed her. She had been so busy with her guests that she had not had time to enjoy the champagne except for the sip she took as she toasted her staff and the success of the Sans. Now, she savored the fruity flavor as she finished the glass with a large gulp. She immediately held out the glass for a refill and smiled up at Ted mischievously as she leaned back onto his chest. Sensing that Karen was shivering slightly in the cool night breeze, Ted removed his dinner jacket with a flourish and placed it over her bare shoulders, moving away from her as he did. She smiled up gratefully. "You always seem to know what I need," she said, wishing that he had stayed close. It had been too long since Robert had held her without expecting something in return. She was more intensely aware of the difference in the two men than she wanted to be. Had she accepted Robert for her husband because the wealth and glamour were more important to her than she had realized? Was she that shallow? No. Certainly there was something more that had attracted her to Robert, something that she could no longer find but that had been there in the beginning.

Karen's discomfort was apparent. She desperately wanted Ted to kiss her but she was not going to give up on her marriage that easily. When Karen said "till death do us part" she meant it, and she would gladly sacrifice her own happiness if that were the right thing to do. But was it right? She had heard the rumors about Robert's affairs but was still not ready to accept the fact that he was running around. Her heart refused to accept what her head already knew. She prayed that Ted would be there for her if the rumors turned out to be true and she was forced to end her marriage.

The sight of Karen slumped against him and trembling from the cold brought Ted back to reality. "Let's hit the sack and get an early start in the morning," Ted said, taking the empty glass from her hand and helping her to her feet.

"That sounds good to me. I don't remember the last time that I felt this tired. You don't mind, do you?"

Ted squeezed her hand tightly in response and walked her all the way to the door of her bedroom, keeping his arm around her shoulder. "See you in the morning, champ," he said as he sadly watched her walk into the bedroom that she shared with Robert. Desperately needing to follow her, he wanted to beg her to stop wasting her life with such a loser and marry him instead. But he knew better. Karen was loyal if anything. She would have to make her own decision to leave Robert before Ted could even think of making a move. If he jumped the gun, Karen would cling to Robert even tighter. Ted knew that he had to be patient, but his heart had its own ideas.

Backtracking down the stairs, Ted rounded through the house, locking doors and shutting lights. A bottle of rum caught his attention, and he snatched it up before making his way back to his room. He knew that he would need it to get through the long night that stretched ahead. Sleep would be impossible with Karen just down the hall.

As soon as he closed the door to the guestroom, Ted poured a full glass and took a long swallow. Exchanging his party clothes for a pair of sweats, he opened the door to the patio and felt the full force of the fierce storm coming in off the water. The wind was brutal as he walked out into the darkness and braced himself against the railing. His eyes strained to see the waves crashing below, but nothing was visible except for the few seconds when lightning shot across the sky and into the water. It looked like it was going to be an exciting night, but this was not the type of excitement that Ted needed. His excitement was sleeping a few feet down the hall.

Chapter Eleven

Karen was out on the main patio when Ted dragged into the kitchen in the morning. He found the cups and poured himself a cup of black coffee before joining her outside.

"Did you sleep well?" he asked as he walked out to the patio.

"Like a baby," she replied. "I'm really surprised since I usually toss and turn all night. But last night was different, and thank God for that. The stress of the opening really exhausted me. I just don't know what I'd do if the Sans failed."

Ted walked over and sat down next to Karen. He put his arm around her shoulders, looked into her sad eyes, and said, "The Sans is not going to fail, and you know it. How could it? You are giving your patients everything they need to recuperate and regain their health in the most beautiful environment known to man. The patients can't help but feel better here."

Karen smiled up at Ted feeling so safe and so grateful for his support, but the feeling was short-lived. Guilt hit her as she realized that she didn't even miss Robert. Her heart knew that there was something fatally wrong with her marriage when she was less lonely when her husband was thousands of miles away. She had obviously married the wrong man. Why hadn't she married someone kind and thoughtful like Ted? Her face flushed with the thought, and she immediately jumped up to get more coffee. "How about some breakfast?" she asked.

"I think I could force myself to eat something if you insist," Ted replied, following Karen into the kitchen. As Karen whipped up western omelets and popped the wheat bread into the toaster, Ted set the table and prepared mimosas. The two of them sat together in comfortable silence as they ate and enjoyed the beautiful morning.

The phone rang just as they were finishing their meal, and Karen reluctantly answered. It was Robert, as she had feared. He asked about the opening and about the party. Karen's answers were perfunctory and brief. She knew Robert did not expect more. He made excuses that he needed to run to a business lunch and hung up with his usual "love you."

As Karen suffered through her conversation with Robert, Ted began cleaning up the table and loading the dishwasher. The amount of commotion let Karen know that Ted was making as much noise as possible as if to avoid overhearing what Karen was saying.

Within a few minutes, Karen rejoined Ted in the kitchen, and they were both strained and silent as they went about finishing the chores. Finally, Karen smiled and asked Ted if he would like to do some sightseeing. Ted agreed, and they parted to go to their separate rooms to dress for the day ahead.

Karen was already out on the patio waiting when Ted emerged from his room. He looked trim and fit in his crisp, white Izod shirt and navy shorts. Karen admired his tanned and muscled legs as she watched him jog into the room. She whistled softly and laughed as he stopped to take a bow. "You sure look good for an old GP. I don't know how your wife ever let you get away. She must have been blind or just plain dumb."

"Sometimes you just don't see what's right in front of your face," Ted said wistfully, and they both knew that he was not referring to his ex-wife.

Before he could continue, Karen grabbed his arm and pulled him toward the front door. "Let's get going. Time's a wasting," she exclaimed as she picked up the car keys and tossed them to Ted. "Let's see what you can do with a real car.

Ted opened the passenger-side door and helped Karen in. He practically ran around to the driver side where he promptly pushed the button to put the top down. He loved driving, and he knew that he was in for a special treat with the Mercedes convertible and its powerful engine. "Where to?" he asked as he peeled out of the driveway and headed for the causeway.

"Just drive, and we'll see where we end up. It's such a beautiful day. We can't go wrong. It will be great no matter where we go. I just love being outside on a day like this."

Ted replied by throwing the car into gear and turning the radio up. The words to an old Drifter's song surrounded them, and they couldn't help but laugh as they both started to sing along at the same moment. Reluctant to break the mood, neither of them said a word to each other for the rest of the drive.

Parking on Front Street a few hours later, Ted opened her door and gently took Karen's hand to help her out of the car. He continued to hold tight to her hand as they explored the town, finally arriving at a small café where they decided to enjoy an early dinner. Karen was suddenly uncomfortable as she prayed that none of Robert's friends would see them. She could imagine the scene if Robert heard that she was walking around town holding Ted Richard's hand. He would be livid.

The café owner came out to greet Miss Karen, as he liked to call her. She was one of his favorite clients, and it showed as he hugged her warmly. "I have the best table for you and your young man, Miss Karen," Milan said as he showed her to a private table set intimately into a dimly lit corner. "I will bring you your usual, on the house of course. And, what will your young man have?"

Karen tried to object to the free wine, saying that it was unnecessary, but Milan simply put his finger to his mouth to silence her. Laughing, Karen signaled her surrender and ordered Black Seal rum on the rocks for Ted.

Milan was back within minutes with a bottle of Australian chardonnay for Karen and a glass of rum for Ted. He chatted amicably as he placed two beautiful crystal wine glasses on the table and poured a full glass for Karen. He looked at her expectantly as he placed the bottle into the ceramic holder filled with ice. Karen sipped the wine with her eyes closed and savored the flavor. When she opened her eyes, she pronounced the wine "magnifico."

"You did it again, Milan. This is wonderful, even better than the one last week. I love the fruity finish and the buttery feel."

Milan was delighted. "You are my best wine critic," he proclaimed. "If you say it is good, I know that all my customers will love it. Now, you two enjoy your drinks, and I will be back in a few minutes to take your order."

Ted looked admiringly at Karen and said, "You didn't tell me that you have another boyfriend. That man just adores you. His eyes actually light up when he looks at you. I think I should be jealous."

"Don't be silly, Ted. He's old enough to be my father. He is just a very kind and generous man. I'm sure he's just as nice to everyone who dines here. It's his way."

"I know. I just like seeing you blush," Ted teased.

Chapter Twelve

The next day, Karen left for the Sans before Ted awoke. Thoughts of Ted occupied her mind as she made the short drive to the Sans. Normally the beautiful scenery would have distracted her, but today she barely noticed. Her attraction to Ted was stronger than she dared to admit. Part of her wished that she had been right there in his bed last night. It had been all she thought about as she drifted off into a restless, dream-filled sleep. Blushing, she thought back to her dream of Ted making love to her on the beach below the house. The sex had been sensual and exciting in her dream, but she could never let it happen in real life. Not as long as she was married to Robert and certainly not as long as she loved Robert. She did love Robert, didn't she? She wanted to believe that she did, but she was no longer sure. The only thing she was sure of was that she would be faithful to him and do her best to make their marriage work. She would not succumb to

Ted's charms as long as her marriage was intact. Feeling guilty for even allowing herself to think about making love with another man, Karen promised herself that she would not let that happen again. She would be faithful to Robert.

A downpour of meetings, rounds, and phone calls drove all wayward thoughts from Karen's mind as she busily passed away the hours at the Sans. Before she knew it, the day was over. It was after six when Karen finally packed her briefcase and started for home. Only then did she allow herself to think about how much she was looking forward to dinner and a quiet night with Ted. A wide smile broke out on her face as she pulled into the driveway, but that smile quickly disappeared when she noticed Robert's BMW parked front and center. What was he doing here? He was not due home for at least another week. With a feeling of dread, she opened the door and walked slowly into the house. Hearing loud male voices coming from the living room, she noted that both Ted and Robert sounded equally strained. She paused to take one last deep breath before forcing a smile onto her face and marching into the living room. Her eyes looked pleadingly at Ted as she hugged and kissed Robert. Ted looked away angrily as Robert made a big show of kissing Karen. The show was obviously for Ted's benefit, since Robert usually barely acknowledged Karen when she came home.

An air kiss and some sarcastic remark construed his normal greeting.

Robert kept his arm around Karen possessively as he invited Ted to join them for dinner at his club. When Karen excused herself to go to the bedroom to change, he made an off-color remark about a quickie and followed immediately. The smile left his face as soon as the door closed behind him. "What the hell is he doing here?" he hissed. "You know that I don't like him. I don't trust him either. What's it going to look like with the two of you here alone? Have you lost your mind?"

Karen knew better than to challenge Robert. He could and would get ugly. She decided to try to placate him instead. "I didn't know that he was coming until he arrived. What could I do? He's all alone. I couldn't just throw him out," Karen said as she put her arms around Robert and kissed him. She could feel Robert respond and felt a shudder escape as he pushed her down onto the bed. This was just the opportunity that Robert had been waiting for as he made sure that Ted could not help but hear the sounds of their lovemaking. She knew better than to object. Instead of crying out in protest, Karen bit her tongue and held back her tears. She knew that Ted had to be aware of what was going on and did not want him to try to interfere. When Robert was like this, the only thing to do was to give him his way. If not, there would be trouble, and Karen did not want Ted to experience Robert's wrath.

Once satisfied, Robert dressed quickly and went to find Ted on the patio. The smirk on his face validated

Ted's impression that the loud sounds from the bedroom were meant to be overheard. His crude comments about Karen's performance were almost more than Ted could bear. Curling his hands into tight fists, he fought to control his temper, but the look in his eyes could not be controlled. It was so hard and so cold that even Robert knew better than to push Ted any further. Turning his back he busied himself pouring two glasses of rum. He silently handed one crystal tumbler to Ted, who downed it immediately and crashed the glass down onto the bar.

Karen heard the crash as she entered the great room and steeled herself for a confrontation. She could not even meet Ted's eyes as she joined the two men a few seconds later. To her surprise, Robert rushed to her side, taking her arm tightly and asking if she wanted a cocktail before they left for dinner. Karen refused, saying that she had a headache and just wanted to go on ahead to dinner before it became worse. She really wanted to crawl back into bed but was afraid that Robert would follow so she forced a smile and asked Ted if he was ready to leave.

Robert didn't seem to notice or care that he was the only one who enjoyed the meal. He ate with obvious gusto as Karen and Ted simply moved the food around their plates, pretending to eat. Ted made up for the lack of food by downing several glasses of rum in quick succession. Robert, for once, kept his thoughts to himself and made small talk about the weather and sports. Neither Karen nor Ted made direct conversation or eye contact with each other until the end of the meal when Robert excused himself to say hello to a wealthy client. Karen smiled hesitantly at Ted as she expressed how sorry she was. Ted just shook his head and looked away angrily. He left the table and paid the check. A few minutes later, Robert and Karen found him sitting on the hood of their car checking e-mail on his Blackberry.

When Ted told the couple that he would be leaving in the morning, Robert smiled his famous fake smile and wished Ted a safe trip home. Karen wanted to object but knew better.

Awakening early the next morning, Karen found the guestroom empty, and Ted gone. Ironically, by the time she got home that night, Robert was also gone. He left a note saying that he had to return to Germany because his big deal was in danger of falling through without his constant supervision. His promise to call her in a few days made Karen furious. She knew that somehow Robert had learned that Ted was here and had only returned home to get rid of him. Robert obviously had his spies watching her and one of them had called him. Now that his mission of getting rid of Ted was accomplished, he was gone again, and Karen was alone as usual.

Chapter Thirteen

Fortunately, Robert had outsmarted himself. Ted was not gone. He had simply taken a room at a neighboring hotel. Surprised and pleased, Karen laughed out loud when Ted called her at work on Friday and asked her to lunch. She turned down the lunch invitation and invited him to dinner at her house instead. Before he could refuse, she let him know that Robert was gone and she was once again alone. Ted accepted her invitation hesitantly. He could not get the memory of the sounds of Robert and Karen in their bedroom the night before out of his mind. The thought of that monster touching her made him physically ill. But he had come all the way from Seattle with a mission, and he was not going to let Robert drive him away.

When Ted arrived shortly before sunset, Karen couldn't help but notice the glow on his face. She attributed it to the sun but Ted would have had the same glow if he had been with her in the middle of an Alaskan winter. The glow came from the feelings he held inside. He was a man in love and it showed.

Karen couldn't deny to herself that she was attracted to Ted, but she would never admit that to him. She hugged him briefly and told him jokingly that he had better be ready to help with dinner tonight. Ted laughed amicably and tousled her hair as he headed for the kitchen.

Anyone looking in the window would have thought that they were watching a long-married couple; Ted and Karen were that comfortable with each other. Words were not necessary as they prepared a simple dinner of grilled fish and salad. Grilled pears in a white wine sauce made the simple but delicious dessert.

Both Ted and Karen were ravenous now that the tension between them had dissipated. They joked and laughed easily as they made their way through their dinner and an entire bottle of wine. Karen added glasses of a dark, delicious port to the tray as she served the simple pear dessert. Ted eyed both admiringly as he dove in with abandonment.

They finished the night with another walk on the beach. As they splashed at the edge of the surf, Ted announced that he would be leaving in the morning. "I hate to go, but I need to get back to my practice," he added.

Karen was disappointed and told him so. Pulling her to him, he stared into her eyes and challenged, "You know what you need to do if you want me to stay." Karen knew only too well but pretended that she didn't. She told him that she would miss him and asked him to think about returning after Christmas when Robert would be away again on business. Promising to think about it, Ted reluctantly turned back toward the villa.

Neither Karen nor Ted slept that night. They both lay awake thinking about each other, only too aware that less than fifty feet of darkness was all that separated them. Karen was finding it hard to deny that she was in love with Ted, and the thought scared her thoroughly. Robert would never allow it. She belonged to him, and he would sooner see her dead than with Ted. Robert could never be allowed to recognize the depth of her feelings for Ted or it would be dangerous for both of them. Robert had never harmed her, but she sensed that he had the capacity to be cruel if he were pushed to that point. It was not worth taking that chance no matter how much she wanted to be with Ted.

Chapter Fourteen

The next few months at the Sans flew by pleasantly and without incident. Hundreds of patients came for treatment and left extolling the virtues of the facility and its non-physician staff. The Sans was a huge success, and everyone was thrilled…everyone except the American medical community that is. The powerful AMA and its members were anything but thrilled. They hated the Sans and everything it stood for. A hospital without physicians? What could be more ridiculous? They had expected the Sans to crash and burn on day one. Total failure was the only viable option for them. But the Sans did not fail. No patients died. No one complained or filed law suits. In fact, just the opposite occurred. Everyone praised the staff and the care that they provided. Patients were treated, got better, and returned to the States to tell others about the Sans. Now the physicians were worried. If the Sans was successful, it could spell the end of the medical profession as they knew it. If the American public ever came to accept medical care without physicians, the entire power structure could change overnight.

As most people were preparing for Thanksgiving and the advent of the holiday season, a group of wealthy, powerful physicians were conspiring by phone to plan a different type of celebration. They were known to each other only as "the partners." The senior partner and non-physician founder of the group was the only one who knew everyone's real names and credentials, and he did not disclose any of his personal information to the others. He had invited each of the other partners based on each candidate's degree of wealth, power, and hatred of Karen and the Sans. Anonymity was assured through the use of conference calls hosted by the senior partner. On this, the last weekend before Thanksgiving, the partners were planning the New Year's celebration that would come with the failure of the Sans. Complicated plans were being formulated that would guarantee that the day of celebration would come. These were the plans that would sabotage the Sans' computer system and cause the deaths of several patients. The deaths were unfortunate but acceptable—collateral damage. This was a small price to pay to put these infidels out of business and to secure the position of physicians as the owners and controllers of all healthcare worldwide and forever more.

Dr Arnold D'Benedectis was the partners' secret weapon. His extensive knowledge of computer systems made him the perfect person to foil the Sans information systems. His forged credentials and bogus résumé had led to his position as the assistant chief information officer at the Sans. As is usual in most hospitals, the role of Carl Guyler, the chief information officer, was that of an administrator and a politician and not a hands-on position. Although, in Carl's case, he was imminently qualified to do both. He had an extensive background in information systems that spanned three decades. In fact, Carl had led the teams that developed the original programs for medication management, remote monitoring, and computer-directed robotic surgery. He was considered to be the foremost authority in the world of healthcare informatics. Despite all his accomplishments, Carl had one shortcoming—his lack of confidence. He would modestly step back and allow others on his team to receive the credit for his work. Preferring to remain in the background, he allowed others to take the glory and the risk. The fear that he would make a mistake and cause a patient's death paralyzed him so much that he no longer touched the computers himself. As unreasonable as the fear was, it nevertheless kept him restricted to his office. Leaving all of the daily operations in the hands of Dr. D'Benedectis, he busied himself with the myriad of administrative duties that come with running a busy hospital information systems department. This was fine with Dr. D., as Dr. D'Benedectis insisted on being addressed. It made it so easy for him to plant the cloaked program that would attack the basic system and change the commands from protocols meant to cure patients to protocols meant to kill them. It was an ambitious plan totally worthy of a mad genius.

Even before opening day, Dr. D. had started to introduce the cloaked viral programs. He buried them deep in the infra-structure to defy detection. His reputation as a loner and an eccentric allowed him to work without suspicion at night after everyone had gone home. Actually his abrasive personality made his employees very glad that he was not at the Sans during the day. Even the chief, Carl Guyler, was relieved not to have Dr. D. around. Carl respected Dr. D.'s reputation but found that he could not respect the man. There was something about Dr. D. that made Carl uncomfortable.

First there was the fact that the man insisted on being called Dr. at all times. This was unusual at the Sans where no one stood on formality or used fancy titles. That was the beauty of the Sans. By eliminating medical doctors, Karen had also eliminated the constant tension that exists in most hospitals where doctors believe that they are above the rules and certainly above all of the other employees. The god syndrome cannot coexist in a collegial, team-friendly environment, and most physicians cannot exist without the god syndrome. They don't mind the team concept as long as they are the undisputed captains of the teams. At the Sans, everyone on the team was equally important and everyone's opinion was respected and considered. Dr. D. just didn't fit into this environment, and Carl knew that it would not be long before he would need to address this problem. He only hoped that Dr. D. would finish debugging all of the software before he was forced to let him go. It would be very difficult for anyone else to step in at this point and take over.

Months of work would need to be repeated, and each program would need to be retested. Carl just did not have the time or the confidence to take on this task at this point especially given the fact that Dr. D. had not allowed anyone to assist him. His insistence on doing all of the testing and debugging alone was quirky but not unheard of in the computer programming community. Many computer geeks live in their own programming world and are particularly introverted. Since Dr. D. was both a medical doctor and a computer geek, it was not surprising that he trusted no one and preferred his own counsel.

Having finished all the program debugging and testing, Dr. D.'s nightly work now consisted of planting the secret commands that he would activate remotely when the time was right. Even this was just about done. Another day or two and he would be ready.

The partners' plan called for Dr. D.'s sudden resignation just before the sabotage program became active on New Year's Eve and when they knew that Carl would be hard pressed to find someone to replace him. They counted on Carl to allow the younger programmers to fill in until someone new could be hired. Although they were bright and well trained, their lack of experience would prevent them from finding the commands Dr. D. had implanted deep into the system. Assuming malfunction, they would suggest shutting down the primary systems and switching to the backups which was exactly what Dr. D. wanted. The backup systems were implanted with even more secret commands that were far more brutal than the ones in the primary. If it got this far, patients would die. The Sans' staff would be blamed, and the public outcry would demand the hospital's closure during the investigations that would certainly ensue. That was the beauty of the scheme. The commands that he had planted would never be found. The cloaked system was undetectable and had been programmed to self-destruct on the execution of a remote command if that became necessary. Computer malfunction would never be proven. Instead, it would appear that the staff was at fault. The staff would be accused of putting the wrong commands into the computers, and their competence would be challenged along with the very idea of allowing non-physicians to direct patient care. The Sans would be destroyed, and the idea of hospitals without doctors would be put to rest forever.

Chapter Fifteen

Thanksgiving was uneventful for Karen. Robert flew into Bermuda on the Wednesday night before the holiday claiming that he was working on a very important project and could barely tear himself away even for just a day or two. His return flight was scheduled to leave Bermuda again on Friday morning. Actually, Karen would have preferred that he had not come home at all. Their relationship had become strained and uncomfortable for Karen since the episode with Ted. Robert didn't even seem to notice, or maybe he just didn't care. Karen didn't know which, and frankly she didn't care much either.

"What time are our dinner reservations?" Robert asked as he walked into the living room on the night before Thanksgiving There was no hug, no kiss, and no "hello" at all. It was as though he had just left the room for a few minutes and was resuming a conversation left mid-sentence.

Karen replied coldly, "I missed you, too, Robert. I'm so glad that you're home."

"Of course I missed you. After all of these years, do I still have to say that all of the time? Why are you so damned insecure? When are you going to grow up?" Robert growled.

Before Karen could reply, Robert's cell phone rang, and he answered on the first ring. "This is business," he said, looking at the caller ID. "I'll take it in the den. Why don't you get ready? I'm starving," he barked over his shoulder as he quickly left the room.

Karen started to follow him but stopped when she heard him saying into the phone, "Don't be angry. You know that I would much prefer to be with you if I could. I hate her, and I can't stand being here without you."

As the door slammed behind Robert, Karen turned back to the living room and sank down on the couch, stunned. Could she have heard correctly? Was Robert having an affair? She felt numb. She just couldn't work up any emotion. Neither hurt nor anger was in her. Could it be that she just didn't care about Robert anymore? Would it actually be a relief if he left permanently? Karen shook her head and stood up. She would get her wrap and her purse. She was not going to deal with this now. She must have heard incorrectly. Robert was not having an affair. He was too preoccupied with his work and lacked the time or emotion for anyone else. He barely had either for Karen, and she was his wife.

When Robert returned to the living room, Karen was smiling valiantly. She walked over and hugged him warmly. "I'm sorry, hon. I guess I'm just a little tired and stressed out," she said, as she kissed him. "Let's go and have a nice dinner. I made reservations at the Hearth. I know that it's your favorite."

Robert simply accepted her apology and took her arm stiffly as he escorted her to her car. He politely opened the passenger door for her and then practically shoved her in. Positioning himself behind the wheel of Karen's car, Robert tuned the radio to his favorite station and turned up the volume, indicating that there would be no further conversation.

Dinner at the Hearth was saved by the sudden appearance of Jorge, one of Robert's close friends. Robert spied Jorge walking through the front door and immediately confronted him. He invited Jorge to join them without any regard for Karen, and the rest of the evening consisted of gentlemanly business and sports talk. Karen was completely ignored as she sat watching the interaction between Jorge and Robert. Karen noted how animated Robert could be when he was with his friends and sadly remembered a time when he was like that with her, too. Back then he would have wanted to have dinner alone with her. Now they were both relieved and happy to have company.

Karen was even more grateful for the distraction since it allowed her the luxury of thinking about Ted. Wondering where he was tonight and with whom he would be spending the evening she felt her face redden as the thought of Ted with another woman sprang to

Sans Docteur Hospital

her mind. Suddenly, she realized that she would be heartsick if he found someone new. She wanted to be the new woman, the only woman in Ted's life, even though that was so unfair while she was still married to Robert. Lost in her thoughts of Ted, Karen suddenly realized that Robert had asked her a question and was waiting for an answer. Embarrassed in front of his friend, he gave Karen the stony look that signaled trouble to come. Forcing a smile, she took his hand as she apologized to Jorge and explained that she was preoccupied by her plans for tomorrow's holiday dinner and all of the tasks that were yet to be done. Robert abruptly signaled the waiter for the check and dinner was over. He didn't even bother to help her with her chair or her wrap as they prepared to leave. His obvious anger made her know that she would pay for her lack of attention later.

    Robert smiled stiffly and wished the restaurant staff a happy holiday as he walked out of the restaurant with Jorge. Radiating charm, he hugged his friend and pumped his hand in a warm manner. Something whispered into the other man's ear caused them both to laugh heartily. Instinctively knowing that the joke was at her expense, Karen walked behind the two men and waited her turn to say good-bye. When the two men parted, Karen moved in to give Jorge her hand and wish him a happy holiday. As he bent over to hug her, she realized that Robert was already getting into the car. She had to run to catch up with him and jump into the car before he took off. As it was, she was barely in the car when he gunned the motor and threw the expensive car into gear, peeling out of the driveway with tires screeching. Karen fell back into the seat as the door slammed, just missing her fingers that were on the door jam. She wanted to scream at Robert and call him a fool, but she knew that she needed to bite her tongue and hold her words if she wanted to be spared his wrath.

Robert was silent in the car on the way home and went immediately to his study when they entered the house. Karen heard him talking quietly into his cell phone as he slammed the heavy study door. Hurriedly, she changed and crawled into bed. Shutting the lights and pulling the covers up around her, Karen willed herself to be sound asleep before Robert came to bed. Despite the tension, she pretended to snore softly when she felt him pull back the covers and sit heavily on his side of the bed. If he knew that she was faking, he obviously didn't care. Turning his back to Karen, he yanked the covers to his side of the bed and was snoring loudly minutes later.

When she knew it was safe, Karen got out of bed quietly and escaped to the patio. Listening to the sound of the waves crashing below, she realized that the time was coming for her to confront Robert. They couldn't go on like this. Her heart told her that he must have someone else. But, appearances were important to Robert and he would never want an embarrassing divorce. He would rather go on living this illusion. It suited him to have his proper wife in Bermuda and a mistress in who knows where. Suffering a sudden rush of emotion, Karen felt sorry for herself, sorry for Robert, and most of all sorry for this mistress. She had no idea what she had gotten herself into.

Chapter Sixteen

When Karen arrived at work early Monday morning, her secretary, Maureen, commented that she looked pale and tired and asked if she felt well. Karen just said that she must have caught a bug and went to her office and closed the door. It wasn't like her to lie to Maureen, but she couldn't discuss Robert while she felt so confused. When she married Robert, she had truly believed it would be for life. "Till death do us part" meant something to Karen. That was the way it was supposed to be. Still valiantly trying to convince herself that she loved Robert, Karen knew that, in their own way, they did love each other. But, they were certainly not in love with each other. For Robert it was a convenience and a matter of ownership and propriety. Proper people simply did not divorce. They always gave the appearance that they were happily married people, no matter how unhappy they were. Appearances were everything and people of his class simply endured and made do for life.

Robert would be the first to admit that his relationship with Tina had started as a matter of making do, but his son was an altogether different matter. Robert had not been prepared for how much he would come to love William. If he and Karen had been able to have children it might have been different. But, as it was, William would be his only heir and legacy when he left this world behind. Tina had changed the stakes when she gave birth to William. William was the future of the Jorgensen name and fortune. He might be illegitimate, but Tina had made sure that he knew who his father was and that the Jorgensen name was his. At some point Robert would need to deal with this, but he was not yet ready. If Karen suspected that he was not entirely faithful, he was sure that she expected that he was engaging in one-night stands. Karen would never believe that he was capable of loving someone at a lower station in life, but Robert did love his mistress and his son in a way that he had never loved Karen. But no matter. Karen was unimportant in the greater scheme of things. Robert would soon be free to live the life he wanted. He would marry Tina and adopt William as his own. Karen would be gone, and Robert would be the grieving young widower. Who could blame him for moving on and trying to make a decent life for himself?

Karen busied herself answering e-mails and phone calls for the rest of the morning. Meetings took the afternoon, and before she realized it, the day was over. The sky grew dark and stormy, and Karen felt the same way inside. This weather suited her mood, and she enjoyed watching the lightning and listening to the thunder. When she finally looked at her watch, she was surprised that it was well past seven. Reluctantly, she gathered her purse and briefcase and made her way to her parking space. Her Mercedes was sitting in space number one, as always. After twenty years of having to walk blocks to find her car, she finally had a space of her own right outside the door. This was so important to her that she made sure that all of her Sans' staff had parking spots in the monitored lot directly adjacent to the hospital.

Leaving the Sans' parking lot, Karen drove slowly through the rainy night. The roads were tricky in the dark, especially after crossing the causeway and traveling down North Shore Road where she lived. A sigh of relief escaped as she pulled into her familiar driveway and jumped out of the car. She threw open the front door and had just rushed inside when a deafening clash of thunder made Karen suddenly wish that Ted were here with her. After checking the phone messages and noting that Robert had not called, Karen changed into a comfortable jogging suit and went to the kitchen to prepare something for dinner. A few sips of wine calmed her nerves as she sat at the kitchen window, mesmerized by the storm moving out over the water. When the oven alarm signaled that the broiled lemon shrimp was ready, she quickly tossed a salad to complete the meal. She preferred to eat simply when Robert was away since he always insisted on formal meals when he was home. Karen was just about to take her first bite when the phone rang. She was surprised and delighted when Ted's voice came booming out of the phone. "Hey, kid. How are you?" Ted asked.

"I'm fine. How about you?" Karen replied.

"What's going on? Since when are you so formal with me?" asked Ted.

"I'm just a little on edge. There's a hell of a storm going on here, and you know how I hate to be alone in a storm!" Karen was sorry as soon as the words left her mouth. She really didn't want Ted to know that Robert was gone again.

"Where the hell is that husband of yours now? Doesn't he ever stay home?"

"Ted, don't. You know that Robert has to travel for his business. Don't make a big deal about it. I'm a big girl. I can take care of myself."

"I know that you hate storms and that you shouldn't be there all alone. I wish I were there with you. I really miss the beach, and I love nothing more than a good storm over the ocean. I had a great time when I was there."

Karen was impressed. Ted usually hated to leave home. "How about coming back soon?" she invited.

"I'm thinking about it," was Ted's surprising answer.

Karen decided not to press the issue and made small talk for a few minutes before hanging up. She felt restless and unsettled after Ted's call, but she had no idea why. She simply attributed it to the weather. Later in bed, her thoughts kept returning to Ted, and she found it difficult to sleep. When she finally did fall into a fitful sleep, she dreamt of making love to Ted. The dream turned into a nightmare when Robert arrived and found them together in bed. Robert was just about to shoot Ted in her dream when a loud bolt of thunder woke her with a start. She was still shaking as she stepped into the shower and tried in vain to drown the memory from her mind. The nightmare continued to haunt her throughout the morning, causing her to feel nervous and jumpy as she drove to the Sans in the pouring rain.

Chapter Seventeen

Carl Guyler and Dr. D. had their routine monthly meeting early on Monday morning. Dr. D., who was never at his best in the morning, was even more disagreeable than usual. Both men looked relieved when Carl's secretary interrupted them to announce that he was late for his next meeting. Dr. D. simply got to his feet and left the room. He never bothered with the amenities that were important to other people. He didn't give a damn. He was just glad to be free of Carl.

Quickly navigating the hallways to his office, Dr. D. reviewed the programming and hit the command that would change the Sans' computers from their medicinal mode to their killer mode. It was time for a test run. Within hours, patients would start to crash. At first, the patients would simply stop receiving the appropriate mediations for short periods of time. Just enough time would elapse to cause blood pressures to rise or fall, pain to increase, and breathing to become labored. As soon as the alarms started to sound, a trigger would cause all medication delivery to return to normal. The interference would be almost impossible to detect. Later, when the time was right, things would heat up even more, and after all of the initial commotion, the patients would start to die undetected. Dr. D. had programmed the monitors that should detect the patients' respiratory and cardiac arrhythmias to turn off for a short period of time. Alarms would be silent as the patients took their last labored breaths.

The first alarm sounded just as Barbara Geraci was starting her daily rounds. She immediately responded to the bedside of an elderly male patient who was agitated and obviously in pain. "What's happening here?" she asked the nurses and ARNPs in the room.

"I don't know," replied the charge nurse. "He's been receiving continuous sedatives and pain medication and was actually bordering on unconsciousness an hour ago. All of a sudden, he woke up and began pulling off his leads and screaming in pain. It's seems as though he stopped getting his medications, but all of the pump settings look fine. The only odd thing is that there is more medication in the bags than what is indicated on the pumps. I'm going to give him a bolus and change the pumps. I'll have medical instrumentation check and see if there was a malfunction." As she spoke, she injected mediation into the patient's IV line, and the patient began to visibly relax.

Barbara noted that the patient wore the orange band that indicated that he was a "no-code" patient, meaning that he was not to be resuscitated if his heart or breathing stopped. "This is no way to die," she said to the staff. "Please get him comfortable and squared away before his family arrives. They would be very upset to see him suffering. This is not the Sans' way."

Before Barbara could say more, she heard another alarm sounding down the hall. She hurried off and found that another patient's heart monitor was setting off the alarm because the patient's heartbeat had slowed precipitously. The staff was busy injecting a medication and applying the external pacemaker that would speed the patient's heart back to normal levels. She decided not to bother them now. She would return later for a detailed explanation.

By the end of her rounds, Barbara was exhausted. Five more patient alarms had sounded as the patients experienced life-threatening anomalies. *What is going on here*, she thought. Nothing like this had ever happened at the Sans, and it needed to be reported immediately. She didn't even stop to acknowledge Karen's secretary, Maureen, as she hurried past her desk and into Karen's office. Karen looked up as Barbara rushed in, but she did not stop talking on the phone. She was visibly upset, and she shook her head from side to side as she said good-bye into the phone and hung up. "I know," she said before Barbara could say a word. "I just called Carl. We need to check every computer and every pump in the building. All of the patients' pump volumes are off from the actual volumes. The pumps must have shut down. Thank God for the monitors and the quick response from the staff. We could have lost those patients. But I can't figure out how it happened. Why those seven patients and not the others? They are all on the same computer system. The only explanation I can think of is that the pumps malfunctioned. We're checking everything right now. Can you speak with the staff and see if anyone noticed any pump problems before the alarms went off? We should probably put extra staff on for the night as well. See how many nurses can work overtime and call in the per diem staff."

Barbara hurried out without saying a word. She knew that Karen wouldn't rest until she got to the bottom of this.

Carl Guyler had all hands on deck with the entire staff checking the pumps and the computer programs. Even Dr. D. was there helping. But, despite all their efforts, they came up empty. They couldn't find anything wrong with the pumps or the computers and were completely stumped. Dr. D. offered to run a special debugging program overnight, just in case they had missed something, and Carl gratefully accepted his suggestion since he couldn't think of anything else to do.

Karen and Carl both decided to stay overnight at the Sans. There were small apartments on site that were used for on-call staff and visitors, and Karen kept one reserved for her use when she had late-night or early-morning meetings. After showering and changing into scrubs, Karen checked the fridge and the cupboards and was pleased to find the makings for a cheese omelet. She poured a cup of coffee as she waited for the eggs to cook. Unable to get her mind off the problem at the Sans, she agonized over what had happened. There were so many safeguards built into the computer applications that it should have been impossible to experience the problems that had surfaced today. So why wasn't it impossible? Why had seven patients come so close to losing their lives? Something was just not right. It didn't add up. Karen had a nagging feeling that she couldn't pinpoint. Her thoughts kept going to Dr. D., but she didn't know why. Could he have something to do with this disaster? Karen's conservative side told her that she was being foolish. A physician like Dr. D. would never do something that would endanger patients. No matter how tired and stressed she was, she couldn't let her dislike for Dr. D. cloud her thinking. There had to be a simple explanation for this problem.

After picking at her omelet, Karen cleaned up and took a glass of milk into the bedroom. She tried to sleep but found it impossible. Instead she watched the all-night movie channel until her alarm went off at 5:00

a.m. Relief washed over her as she realized that the phone had not rung during the long night. Thinking that this was a good omen and that there would be no further problems, Karen felt her mood lighten as she showered and dressed for the day.

Karen found the administrative suite full when she arrived. Her secretary, Maureen, was there and had already placed a cup of coffee on Karen's desk. Barbara, John, and Carl were also there and were completing a patient review on her computer. Dozens of pieces of paper had already spit out of the printer, and more were following. Karen picked up the printouts and placed them on her desk. As she sipped her coffee, she studied them closely. Complete information on the current inpatients unfolded on Karen's desk. Each printout contained the medical orders on one side and the actual medication administered during the night shift on the other. Karen compared each carefully and was relieved to see that all matched perfectly. Just as she finished the review, Karen smiled up at Barbara and Carl. "It's all okay," she said.

"We know," Barbara replied. "We also knew that you wouldn't be happy until you saw for yourself. We know you too well."

Karen laughed and shook her head. "I can't help it, you guys. You know that I trust you, but it makes me feel better to actually be doing something. I feel so helpless when it comes to computer issues. I wish I knew more."

"It wouldn't help. I know as much as anyone, but I'm completely stumped on this one. There is absolutely no reason for what happened yesterday. I would say it was impossible if I hadn't been here to see it for myself," Carl lamented as he sat down on the couch.

Barbara, ever the pragmatist, suggested that they all get back to work. "There are patients to be cared for out there. Let's leave this to the computer geek and get back to business."

"You shouldn't call him that," said Karen, knowing that Barbara was referring to Dr. D.

"He is a geek, and I'm being kind. I could call him much worse. I even heard him say something yesterday about incompetent clinical staff always blaming the computers for their foul ups."

"Is this true, Carl?" demanded Karen

Carl scowled at Barbara. "You know how he is. He always thinks that he knows better than anyone else. What can I do? He's the best we have, and I can't afford to upset him."

Karen disagreed. "You are the best we have, and I expect you to keep him under control. He is supposed to be mentoring the others and teaching them the programs. I don't want to be at his mercy should he decide to make more demands. He's already a prima donna. I don't know why you put up with his bullshit. You are ten times better than he will ever be."

"Karen, I wish you were right but you're not. You know that I don't have the expertise that he has. I could never have created this program on my own. I'm not even certain that I could maintain it without his help," Carl replied.

Karen was obviously distressed by Carl's comments. "Then, you better get up to speed, Carl. I can't promise you how much longer we can put up with his attitude. Remember that most of our staff works here because they wanted to get away from doctors with the god syndrome. I don't want to lose any of them. Please do something with him."

Carl grunted and walked out, shaking his head.

Chapter Eighteen

Barbara and Karen proceeded to make their morning rounds throughout the hospital and were both relieved to see that everything seemed to be back to normal on the units. The staff was obviously on edge and was even more diligent about double-checking the computers and the pumps, but all seemed to be as it should.

After making the final rounds of all of the inpatient units, Karen breathed a sigh of relief and left for home, leaving strict instructions to call her immediately if anything went wrong. She was profoundly tired and felt in the need of some comfort food so she decided to stop at Moon's Tavern for a quick dinner. She loved the location on Walsingham Bay near the Crystal Caves. Her favorite table was close to the back fireplace where she could enjoy the fire as she savored the yellowtail. Bruno spotted her immediately as she entered. He took her arm as he walked her to her favorite table. "Is Robert joining you tonight, Mrs. Jorgenson? "

"Please call me Karen, and no, Robert is out of town."

"Well, no matter. I will make sure that you are well cared for in his absence. Please have a seat." He snapped his fingers at one of the waiters as he pulled Karen's chair and sat her at the table. "Get Mrs. Jorgensen a glass of the best Chardonnay right away. Will it be the usual tonight?"

Karen smiled and shook her head wearily. Immediately, the waiter returned with her glass of wine and a covered basket of fresh, hot bread. Karen normally abstained, but tonight she took a large slice of bread and slathered on the flavored butter. She actually felt herself begin to relax as she sipped her wine and enjoyed her bread and salad. By the time she finished her dinner, she was feeling very tired. The past several nights of poor sleep were taking their toll on her. She knew that she needed to get home before drowsiness overtook her to the point that it would be unsafe to drive. Signaling the waiter wearily, Karen signed the check, charging the meal to Robert's account, and walked slowly to her car. She took several deep breaths of the sea air before starting the short drive back to her house. She loved driving around Bermuda and was so grateful that they had found the property just off North Shore Road in Hamilton. It was the perfect location for their villa—private and secluded but breathtakingly beautiful. The fact that it was just over the causeway from the airport and the Sans made the trip to work an enjoyable adventure every morning.

Upon entering the great room, Karen automatically checked for messages. It was a habit developed over twenty-plus years of being on-call for numerous hospitals. She mentally noted that Robert had still not called. His silences were becoming longer and longer. There had been a time when he had called several times a day. Now she was lucky if he called once in several days. It was mildly annoying but not really distressing. She knew that her own feelings had changed over the years. What had started as love was now something else. She was not sure how to describe her feelings for her husband. It was almost a lack of feeling, a void that was enlarging with every day that passed. One of these days they were going to have to deal with this. They would be forced to admit to each other that this marriage was in name only. They either needed to work to get back what they once had or recognize that it was time to say a final good-bye. Which would Robert want? What did she want? *It is all too much to think about tonight*, she thought as she changed into jogging clothes for her nightly walk along the beach. She loved the isolation of the beach at night with the moonlight reflecting off the crashing waves.

After a long relaxing walk, Karen's mood had lightened. She showered quickly and settled comfortably into her big four-poster bed feeling tired but content. This was the best she had felt in months. Little did she know that this was just the calm before the storm.

Sans Docteur Hospital

As Karen slept, Dr. D. worked. It was time to program the big assault. They had not heeded his first warning. They would not ignore the next one, not when patients started to die at the Sans. He knew that Karen and the Bermuda government would receive the final warning in the next few days. He wasn't privy to the exact wording, but he could guess. Patients had come close to dying because of the incompetence of the staff at the Sans. Karen should transfer the patients to King Edwards, the only other hospital on Bermuda, and close the doors to the Sans immediately. Otherwise, the information about the computer malfunctions would be made public and released to the international press corps. It would be a public relations nightmare. The partners would make sure of that.

Dr. D. completed his program just as the sun was rising. Hurrying, he packed up and left before the day shift staff started to arrive. He found them so annoying as they went through their daily activities of checking the systems while never realizing that there were two systems running. Thinking of the chaos that would happen when he activated his killer program, he couldn't help but chuckle.

Chapter Nineteen

The final threatening notice arrived on Christmas Eve; however, Karen was so busy with the hospital celebrations that it sat unopened in her in-box, buried under tons of Christmas cards and junk mail. As soon as the parties were over, Karen left for home. She was hosting Robert's family and his friends for Christmas dinner tomorrow, and she still had several last minute preparations to make. Rushing from her office, she hugged Maureen and Barbara and wished them a "Merry Christmas." She started to apologize that she couldn't invite them to her holiday party, but they stopped her quickly and good-naturedly pushed her toward the door. Karen knew that they really didn't want to attend Robert's party any more than Robert wanted them there.

Karen's first stop on the way home was at the wine shop. As soon as she entered, she heard the owner, Sara, call her name. "Karen, I thought you had forgotten to come by. I was just about to call the house."

"I'm so sorry," Karen apologized to her friend. "I was stuck at work later than I expected. I was afraid that you would be closed by the time I got here. I hope I'm not keeping you from closing shop."

"No worries. I know that you are always at that hospital. Don't you ever take time for yourself?" asked Sara.

"Never mind. I hear enough of that from Robert. Give me a break, and just help me pick out the wine and champagne for Robert's dinner tomorrow. What do you think I should get?"

Sara recommended a dry white, a dessert white, and several reds. She also recommended an excellent champagne, but they both knew that Robert would only drink Dom. He was definitely a price snob. Karen took his usual case of Dom, but she also took several bottles of the champagne that Sara recommended. She would drink that when Robert was out of town. He didn't really care what she drank or served to her friends. He considered hospital people to be the equivalent of blue-collar workers and definitely not in his league. He avoided any association with Karen's friends unless it was absolutely necessary, and even then he disassociated himself as much as possible. That was really okay with Karen's friends, who really didn't care for Robert either. They couldn't understand how someone as kind and caring as Karen could have married an arrogant snob like Robert, but they tried to be as pleasant as possible whenever he was present. It wasn't easy, but they wouldn't hurt Karen for anything in the world.

Sara promised to have Karen's order delivered that evening as she hugged Karen and wished her a "Merry Christmas." Karen hugged Sara back and made her promise to come to dinner next week after Robert was gone again. As Sara watched Karen run back to her car, the look of concern on her face was obvious. Karen wasn't happy, and it showed. Everyone knew it, but no one would say anything about it for fear of hurting Karen more.

Karen's good spirit started to sink again as she turned into the driveway and noted that Robert's car was already there. As usual, he had taken the entire space near the entrance, forcing her to park behind him. Karen sighed as she remembered the fight with the Bermuda officials when Robert insisted on the second car. He knew that only one car was allowed per family in Bermuda, but he never thought that rules applied to him. In the end, he had registered his car in his company's name to avoid the hassle, but he still seethed when he remembered that he had come close to not getting his own way. He had never experienced that before. Everything was always Robert's way or no way. He didn't tolerate anything less.

Robert was dressed and waiting when Karen walked in. "Where have you been? We're late. Hurry up and change." Robert gave Karen a half-hearted hug as he practically shoved her toward the bedroom. "I made the reservation at the Hearth. Sean expects us by eight so please hurry."

Karen forced herself to smile as she hurried to the bedroom. She quickly showered and dressed in a new red pantsuit grateful that Robert had stayed in the living room. He was already at the door by the time she finished getting ready. He quickly grabbed her arm and escorted her to the car, scowling when he noted that her car was in the way. "Just give me the keys. I'll drive your car," he ordered Karen. She simply handed over the keys and slid into the passenger seat. "You know how much I hate being late. Why couldn't you have come home earlier?" Robert demanded.

Karen decided to take the easy road and simply apologize. Satisfied, Robert dismissed her and turned his attention to the road. He drove in his usual fashion—speeding and cutting through traffic without any regard for any other cars on the road. He just ignored the other drivers who cussed at him and gave him the finger as he deftly cut them off and sped ahead. Karen was relieved when they reached the restaurant without serious incident.

Sean, the head chef, greeted Robert personally and shook his hand when they entered the Hearth. He escorted them to the best table where Robert's friends were already seated. Robert's best friend, Albert, was the first to speak. "Karen, I don't believe you've met my wife, Heather. She's been dying to meet you. I've been telling her all about you and your pseudo-hospital."

Karen was shocked. She had been close friends with Albert's first wife, Samantha, before he divorced her. She thought that Samantha was a wonderful person with intelligence and a quick wit—traits that were definitely missing in Albert. Karen couldn't believe that Albert had remarried so quickly. It was only two months since the divorce was finalized. And how could he have replaced Samantha with this child standing before her? Trying to smile, Karen stretched out her hand toward Heather. Ignoring it, Heather, quickly hugged her instead. "I've been so anxious to meet you. Albert has told me everything about you. I think what you are doing is very brave. How can you even think of running a hospital without doctors? The patients must be scared to death!" Heather blurted out.

Everyone at the table stopped talking and stared at Karen, waiting for the inevitable explosion. To everyone's surprise, Karen smiled and said, "I'll explain it to you later when you've grown up. Don't worry your little head about it for now."

"Oh, okay," was Heather's only reply. Obviously she didn't even realize that she had been insulted. Albert grabbed her arm and sat her down as Robert did the same to Karen.

The conversation at the table immediately resumed with everyone talking to Robert at once. He was, as always, the center of attention, and he wouldn't have had it any other way. He truly believed that the world revolved around him, and there had been a time when

Karen believed that as well. She couldn't help but shake her head as she remembered how it had been in the beginning. How could she have been so juvenile and naïve and so easily impressed with this man who valued only material things? Perhaps she had been too young to realize that his charm and wit were always at someone else's expense.

In the beginning Karen had thought that Robert was the most wonderful and generous person she had ever met. She didn't realize that his gifts were just his way of controlling her and turning her into the person he wanted her to be. His trophy wife had to have the best of everything or it would reflect badly on him. He bought her the finest jewelry and clothes from the best designers. He sent her to the trendiest boutiques to have her hair and makeup done and when he was finished, Karen no longer even resembled the person she had been when they met. Viewing her as a diamond in the rough, Robert took every opportunity to turn her into his little gem. Fortunately for Karen, the changes were all on the outside. Inside she remained the same kind, caring person she had always been. Over time she found her own style and no longer relied on Robert to make decisions for her. She had good taste, but unlike Robert, she did not feel the need to only buy the most expensive items. He always equated price with quality, but she knew better. Her talent was finding quality at bargain prices. The outfit she wore tonight was exquisite, but if Robert had known that it was a sale item, he would have been furious and accused her of trying to embarrass him in front on his friends.

Lost in these thoughts she suddenly realized that someone was talking to her. The waiter was standing at her side and obviously waiting for her to order. It was a good thing that she knew this restaurant well since she had not even looked at the menu. Quickly ordering a spinach salad and the linguini in red clam sauce, she looked up to find Robert glowering at her. Forcing herself to smile back at him she mouthed a silent "sorry" as she vowed to pay attention to Robert and his friends for the rest of the evening. Good to her promise, she charmed everyone with her bright conversation and good humor. Robert seemed content and quiet on the way home, and Karen was grateful. She was too tired and too afraid of what the outcome would be when they finally dealt with their problems. To her surprise and delight, Robert went to bed immediately when they got home. In fact, he was snoring softly as Karen slid into her side of the big bed. Taking care not to wake him, she tried not to toss and turn as she lay awake, unable to sleep.

Karen was up at dawn, dressed, and working on the final details for the party when Robert appeared looking flawless, even at this time of the morning. He waved his hello as he went into the kitchen to give the cook his breakfast order. As always he was happiest when the cook was here and he didn't need to rely on Karen for his meals. He thought it was beneath him to have his wife prepare her own meals. If he were home more, he would have insisted on full-time help. As it was, they used the cook and the catering services whenever they had company. He didn't care what Karen did in private, but she would not be cooking and serving his friends and family.

Robert enjoyed his breakfast on the balcony, and Karen joined him just as he was finishing. Taking the seat next to him, she poured a cup of coffee for herself and refilled his cup. They sat in silence for the next few minutes with only the sound of the surf hitting the rocks below. Finally Robert wiped his mouth with the napkin and stood up. "I assume that everything is ready for this afternoon?"

"Of course. We are having a light brunch out here on the patio when everyone arrives. The jazz duo that you like so much will play soft, seasonal tunes while we eat. We will then go to the living room to light the tree and open presents. Afterward, our formal dinner will be served in the dining room. You should see it. It looks so beautiful. The decorator and the caterer outdid themselves, and the menu includes all of your favorites—"

"The duck had better be perfect this year. Remember he burnt it last year and ruined the entire dinner," Robert interrupted. "I want everything to be perfect for my parents."

Karen went out of her way to ensure that Robert's parents and friends thoroughly enjoyed the day and the meals. Everything was perfect, and no one voiced even one word of complaint. Even Robert's mother had to begrudgingly admit that the day was nearly perfect, although she added that she was certain that she could have done better herself. She told everyone who would listen that she considered herself the consummate hostess and thrived on elegant social situations. Karen would never be as comfortable in high society. She felt like a girl from the wrong side of the tracks playing dress-up whenever Robert's mother was near.

Relieved that his visit home was almost over, Robert was looking forward to spending a belated Christmas with Tina and William. There was a room full of presents waiting under the tree to be opened after Robert's return.

Actually, Robert was already sitting in Tina's living room, opening presents when Karen awoke the next morning. He had taken an early flight mainly to avoid having to see Karen before he left. A good-bye note on the kitchen counter simply said that he would call when he could. Since he had already told her that he would be in Germany for the New Year's holiday, she knew that it would be weeks before he came home again. He had claimed that he would have invited her to come to Germany for New Year's Eve, but he knew how busy she was at the Sans. Honestly, she was not planning to be that busy, but she didn't argue. She really didn't want to go on a trip with Robert, and she was relieved that she wouldn't have to plan a big showy New Year's Eve party here in Bermuda. She much preferred to spend the last night of the year on her own here, thinking and toasting the New Year. She really didn't mind being alone, and that surprised her. She remembered a time when she would have gone to the other side of the world to be with Robert. When had that changed? She wasn't sure, but she knew why it had changed. Robert had shown his true colors one too many times and had proven to her that he was not the man that she thought she had fallen in love with. She had been a victim of Robert's deceit. In fact, looking back, Karen admitted that she had noticed a change in him at the wedding reception. He had already started to morph back into his real, obnoxious self as he screamed at the wedding planner and called her an idiot because one of the waitstaff had spilled a few drops of champagne on Robert's tux sleeve. Actually, Robert had hit the bottle with his own hand and caused the spillage himself, but that made little difference as he demanded that the young woman be fired immediately.

Chapter Twenty

Karen had slept poorly on the weekend and, as a result, arrived at work late and out-of-sorts on Monday morning. Her secretary, Maureen, took one look at the dark circles under Karen's eyes and headed for the coffee pot. She followed Karen into the office with a steaming cup of hot, dark coffee. Karen smiled weakly and thanked her. She also thanked her silently when she looked at her daily schedule and realized that Maureen had not scheduled any meetings for today. Karen could catch up on paperwork and then make rounds through the Sans, one of her favorite activities. She loved seeing the staff and talking to them informally, and her outlook brightened with anticipation.

Karen was actually feeling much better when Barbara Geraci popped her head through the door. "Hi, ready for rounds?" Barbara asked as Karen waved her in.

"How was your Christmas?" Karen asked. "Did you have your usual rowdy parties?"

"Of course. We had a great time, and we are not rowdy, thank you. We are just boisterous and high-spirited." Barbara laughed. "And how was your holiday?"

"It wasn't bad actually. Robert seemed to enjoy everything I planned, and for once, my in-laws had no complaints. That's a Christmas miracle in itself," Karen quipped as she grabbed Barbara's hand and said, "Come on. Let's get going on rounds before you start psychoanalyzing me again."

Two hours later they were laughing with the nurses on Two-West as one of the nurses told the story of her midnight proposal from her very drunk boyfriend. It seems that he was so nervous that he drank way too much and passed out right in the middle of his proposal. It was a good thing that he was down on one knee and didn't have far to fall. He awoke on the floor the next morning and couldn't remember whether he had proposed or not.

They were still chuckling when they swung into the cafeteria. Karen liked eating in the Sans' café. It was light and airy and decorated in a nautical theme. But more than that, Karen enjoyed the camaraderie. Everyone ate and socialized together. There was no caste system at the Sans. Karen was as likely to eat with someone from housekeeping as she was to be with Barbara or one of the senior staff members. Today they sat with a group of ARNPs as they all enjoyed swapping Christmas stories and plans for the New Year.

Karen thought things couldn't get any better, and unfortunately she was right.

Chapter Twenty-One

The week flew by without incident, and by the day before New Year's Eve, Karen was feeling more relaxed and confident than she had in months. Just as she was settling in to start answering e-mails her secretary buzzed her, delighting her with the news that Ted was on the line. She was even more delighted when he told her that he was thinking of coming back to Bermuda for the New Year's holiday. Since Robert would be away for the next few weeks, Karen had no hesitation in inviting Ted to stay with her. After finalizing the arrangements to pick him up at the airport the next day, she immediately began making plans for the weekend. It looked like it was going to be a happy New Year after all.

On New Year's Eve, Karen drove to the airport with the top down and the wind blowing through her hair. The weather was beautiful, and Karen couldn't remember the last time she had felt this sense of contentment. Her high spirits had a lot to do with Robert's absence and Ted's visit, but she refused to let that bring her down. She was going to enjoy this New Year's Eve after all.

Karen arrived at Bermuda International in St. George with time to spare. She waited impatiently as Ted cleared customs and finally came into view. She could see even from this distance that he looked tired. It had been a long and crowded flight, but there was something more causing the slump of his shoulders and the preoccupied look on his face. Karen immediately started to worry, but the minute Ted caught sight of her, his expression changed. His eyes twinkled and his grin spread from ear-to-ear. Karen couldn't help but laugh as he all but ran to her spot at the back of the crowd. He hugged her a little too tightly and a little too long. As their eyes met, Karen sensed that this trip was going to be different. She looked away and struggled to regain her composure. There was definitely something different in Ted's behavior, and it frightened her.

A few minutes later, they put Ted's luggage in the back of the Mercedes and took off into the afternoon traffic. Karen smiled at Ted brightly. She couldn't believe that he was actually here, and she told him so. For a man who never took vacation, this was his second in as many months. Something was definitely changing. Ted just smiled back smugly and kept his silence.

Sans Docteur Hospital

Not wanting too much idle time on their hands, Karen suggested a horseback ride at South Shore Park. She knew that Ted loved horses and wouldn't be able to resist. It was a perfect time of day for their ride, and they both thoroughly enjoyed it. They loped along in silence, letting the horses take the lead and decide the direction. As the horses slowly headed back for the stables, Karen wondered to herself why she and Robert never enjoyed simple pleasures like this. The answer came to her immediately. Robert didn't enjoy anything simple. He always had to be waited on. He needed to have the best of everything. She couldn't imagine him sitting on one of these smelly old horses in his just-pressed Armani suit and spit-shined Gucci loafers. She actually laughed aloud at the thought. Ted smiled at her and asked her what the joke was, but she simply shook her head and galloped away.

They were both feeling very mellow and content when they pulled into the driveway at the villa. Ted retrieved his luggage as Karen unlocked the front door. "Just make yourself comfortable in the guestroom. You know where it is!" Karen shouted as she went to the back of the house and began opening the patio doors to let the evening breezes in. Deliberately taking her time, she stopped to enjoy watching the seagulls play in the crashing surf. She needed a few private moments to think since she couldn't think straight when Ted was near. Just one whiff of his cologne and she lost all ability to concentrate on anything other than what it would be like to be in his arms. It was all she could do to restrain herself from going to him now. She blushed as she pictured him stepping into the guestroom shower. She blushed even more when she pictured herself stepping in behind him.

Ted returned to the living room after showering and changing into jeans and a polo shirt and was surprised to find that Karen had already lit the fire and turned on her favorite music. She was standing on the patio, looking out at the Atlantic when Ted came up behind her. She jumped when he put his hand lightly on her shoulder. "Wow, why so jumpy?" Ted asked.

"You just surprised me. I didn't expect you back so soon. Robert always takes at least an hour to shower and change."

Ted just shook his head and said, "I'm not Robert."

Karen sighed ruefully and started to apologize again about the fact that she had been unable to get them reservations for the New Year's Eve celebration. Until Ted had called, she had intended to spend a quiet evening alone with a fire and music from a new album by her favorite artist, Andrea Bocelli. Karen loved his Italian arias as much as Robert hated them. She could never really enjoy listening when Robert was home so she was really looking forward to enjoying the new album tonight. Another thing she intended to enjoy was the several bottles of champagne that Sara over at the Wine Cellar had sold her before the holiday. She had intended to pop one open and just mellow out as the old year ended. She was always a little sad to see the end of a year and even more than a little apprehensive about what the New Year would bring. Her apprehension was justified this year. She sensed that many changes were heading her way.

"I'm sorry, but I couldn't get reservations for tonight. I tried every good place in town, and they were all completely booked. If Robert had called I know that they would have found a way to fit us in, but the locals are not all that fond of me. They still don't trust the crazy American woman who is trying to run a hospital without doctors. They—"

Ted cut her off, "I didn't come all this way because I wanted to go to a restaurant. I came to be with you. And, this is perfect. I couldn't ask for more. We have a roaring fire, a beautiful view, great Italian music, and no one to bother us." As if on cue, the ringing of the phone cut through the music. She and Ted both groaned out loud as she hurried to answer. To her great dismay, Robert's voice boomed into the room. Flashing Ted an apologetic look, she walked into the kitchen. "What's all that noise there?" Robert demanded.

"It's not noise. It's Bocelli, and you know it," Karen snapped back.

"Don't be so touchy. I know who it is. I was just kidding. I didn't mean to upset you. I only called to wish you a Happy New Year. I'm sorry that you have to be there alone, but it's not my fault. You should have taken the time off and come with me. I don't like being away from you on the holidays. You know that." Robert actually managed to sound sincere as he went on. "I thought I would call early since I'll be out with my business associates at midnight and may not be able to get a chance to break way. You know how it is. Everyone gets a little crazed at midnight."

Business associates? Karen wondered if she believed that and then realized she didn't care. She was just as glad that he had called now and would not be interrupting her later, but honestly, she would have preferred that he had not called her at all. She felt guilty about letting him believe that she was there alone and not telling him that Ted was here, but there was no way that she was going to get into that with him when Ted was just a few feet away out on the patio. "I'm sorry. I guess I'm just tired and lonely. I miss you, too. Thank you for calling. I hope you have a Happy New Year," Karen said sweetly.

"That's better. I have to run now. I'll call again when I get a chance. Love you."

She was forced to answer, "Love you, too," as she realized that he had already hung up.

Ted cringed as he heard the end of her brief conversation. How could she love a jerk like Robert? He didn't deserve someone like Karen. Ted knew that if he were lucky enough to have a woman like Karen in his life, he would never leave her alone on the holidays or any other time. He would rearrange everything in his life for her and follow her anywhere. In fact, that's exactly what he was doing now. He should be back in Seattle with his practice and his patients, but he just didn't care. Nothing was going to stand in the way of his being with Karen—not his practice and certainly not Robert.

A few hundred miles away, Robert was already making a second phone call. This one made him happier. When he heard a muffled hello, he immediately asked, "Is everything set for tonight? I don't want anything going wrong."

The deep, masculine voice on the other end of the line assured him that all was in place and that the fireworks would begin at midnight. Everyone was ready, and the plan had already begun to roll out. "The Sans will be history before you know it," the voice continued. "Nothing is going to go wrong. You just do your part, and let me take care of the rest. And don't call here again. It's too dangerous. I'll let you know when it's all over."

Robert was angered and replied, "Don't tell me what to do. I know my end. Just make sure that you don't screw this up." He slammed down the phone so hard that William, who had been sleeping in the other room, started to cry. Robert could hear Tina's voice trying to soothe the baby, as he opened the door and stepped into the living room. His entire demeanor changed instantly. "Here, give me the little guy," he said as he put out his arms for William. He put his other arm around Tina and sighed happily. This was all he had ever wanted from life—a beautiful, young wife and a fine son. And both of them totally devoted to him and his happiness. Tina had him convinced that she wanted nothing more than to be his wife and William's mother. Unlike Karen with her lofty ambitions, Tina had told him from the start that she didn't need a career to make her feel fulfilled. She assured him that she already had everything that she needed to make her content, except for the marriage license and the ring on her finger, and Robert had promised that both would soon be hers.

Robert knew that Karen would fall apart after the Sans crashed. Her suicide would be no surprise to anyone who knew how much the Sans meant to her. And once Karen was gone, who would blame him for finding some solace with someone new? After all he was still young and had the best part of his life still ahead of him. He couldn't be expected to mourn forever. His plan would fall into place perfectly. He just had to wait a little while longer.

Chapter Twenty-Two

Just as Bermuda celebrated and welcomed in the New Year, Dr. D.'s diabolic plan began to roll out. As Ted and Karen toasted the New Year and kissed each other on the cheek, things at the Sans started to go awry. Ted gulped down the remainder of his champagne, put down his glass, and took Karen by the shoulders. He looked deep into her eyes and was just about to kiss her on the lips when the phone began to ring again. For a second, neither one moved. They just continued to stare at each other as their hearts beat wildly. Karen willed the phone to stop ringing. She sensed what Ted was about to do, and she didn't want him to stop now. When Karen's beeper started to chime, Karen knew something was definitely wrong. Her stomach lurched and a cold chill ran up her spine as she ran to pick up the phone. Barbara's voice was strained as she told

Karen that she had better get to the Sans right away. The computers were acting up again. They had shut down exactly at midnight, and now that they had come back online, alarms were going off all over the Sans. The computer staff had switched from the primary system to the secondary, but things were only getting worse. It was total chaos. Patients and visitors were in a panic and the clinical staff was trying in vain to maintain some semblance of order. No one knew exactly what was happening, and anxiety was rampant in patients, visitors, and staff alike.

Karen didn't wait to hear more. She dropped the phone, ran into the foyer, grabbed her keys and lab coat and headed for the front door. Ted was right on her heels. Having overheard parts of the conversation, he knew how serious this could be. He had barely closed the passenger-side door when Karen threw the Mercedes into gear and sped out of the driveway. She avoided looking in his direction, shifting swiftly into high gear and quickly passing all cars in her way. He reached over and took her hand as she drove frantically over the causeway. "Don't worry. I'm sure there's a logical explanation. We'll work it out," Ted assured her.

She bravely tried to smile back as she squeezed his hand. "I'm scared, Ted. Something is very wrong. I can feel it. I'm just glad that you are here with me. I might need your help."

They pulled up alongside her private entrance to the Sans and both ran for the door. The minute they were inside, they could hear alarms going off from all directions. As she ran for the computer command station, her heart felt as though it would beat right out of her chest. Barbara and Carl were both in the room with at least a dozen technicians. Carl was sweating and visibly shaking as he frantically punched commands on the keyboard. He screamed for someone to shut off the alarms, and within seconds the room went deathly silent. Looking up at Karen and shaking his head, he announced, "I don't know what's happening. Everything looks fine, but patient alarms are going off all over the hospital. Med pumps have shut down completely, and patients are crashing. Nothing is working properly."

"Okay, Carl, just take it easy. You will figure this out. Where is Dr. D.? Isn't he supposed to be here now? Why isn't he helping?"

"He called out sick," Carl said. "He says that he has the swine flu. He won't be back for a week at least. You know the CDC recommendations."

Karen thought a moment and said, "Call him. Tell him to get down here and clean up this mess. I don't care if he has the flu. He doesn't do patient care. The CDC recommendations don't apply to him. He can just suck it up like the rest of us. Get him here. Now!" she ordered impatiently. One of the chief techs immediately picked up the phone and starting dialing Dr. D.'s number as Karen stood over his shoulder holding her breath. After six rings, Dr. D.'s voicemail picked up, instructing the caller to leave a message. The tech handed the receiver to Karen, and she demanded that Dr. D. pick up the phone. Receiving no reply, Karen instructed Dr. D. to call back immediately, saying that there was an emergency at the Sans and his assistance was urgently needed. She resisted the urge to tell him that if he didn't get in immediately he needn't bother to return at all. It wouldn't do to upset him right now when he was needed so badly. He would be reprimanded harshly after the emergency was resolved.

"Barb, let's get out there and give the clinical staff a hand. We can't do anything more in here." Leaving the room, Karen yelled back over her shoulder, "Carl, when Dr D calls, you tell him to get in here STAT or start looking for a new job. I don't want to hear any excuses. I want to see him here when I get back."

Karen and Barbara were not surprised by the controlled chaos they found out on the floors. The emergency call had gone out at midnight, and each and every staff member had responded immediately. Karen could see that many were still in tuxedos and evening gowns under their lab coats. But they were ultimate professionals as they hurried to take the patients off the computerized systems and silence the alarms. Thank God that the staff had practiced down-time procedures before the Sans opened and knew exactly what to do. Although two patients had coded when everything shut down at midnight, they had both been resuscitated but only one successfully. The first patient, Mr. Simpson, an elderly man with lung cancer, was now stable. The other patient, Cynthia Charles, was not so lucky. She was now comatose, and her condition was critical. The chief nurse anesthetist, Jessica Jenson, and her team of CRNAs were gathered at the bedside, studying the monitor that had now been disconnected from the hospital's computer system. Her blood pressure was dangerously low, and her pulse was weak and irregular.

"I don't know what could have happened," Helen, the chief ARNP, lamented. "She was perfectly stable the last time the staff checked her at 11:00 p.m. She was watching TV and even joked with the nurse who was hanging a new bag of Taxol. The medication in the bag should have lasted for six hours, but at midnight the alarm went off. We found her in complete arrest with an empty bag hanging from the IV pole. How could this happen? The IV pumps are computerized and self-programmed. They couldn't make such a large miscalculation. Could they?"

Tom, her assistant and a self-proclaimed computer geek, was the first to answer. "There's no way this should be happening. These systems are prime. They have more redundancy and safe guards built into them than the entire US Homeland Security system. Something else must be wrong. If you ask me, I think we're dealing with a case of sabotage."

Karen almost cried when she looked down at Cynthia. Why did this have to be happening to her? She had already suffered so much from the treatment she had received back in the States. Her patience during her therapy here had been rewarded just last week when she was told that the treatment was successful and her tumor had shrunk appreciably. She should be going home this week, not lying here close to death. And what about her husband? Senator Brian Charles was going to explode when he heard this news. He didn't like the idea of the Sans one bit and had been against her decision to come here. If his wife died, he would make it his mission to ruin Karen and close the Sans for good.

Before Karen could even think about what she was going to say to Senator Charles, Bruce, the marketing director, burst into the room. "Karen, thank God I found you. You need to come with me. The phones are ringing off the hook. Somehow the press got wind of this, and they are demanding to speak to you. Security just called to say that there are news crews setting up their cameras out front. What are we going to do? This is a disaster!"

Karen allowed herself to be pulled quickly down to her office. She had no idea how the press could have found out about this. Someone had to have called them. But who? She couldn't imagine any of the San's staff calling the press. Maybe one of the emergency phone calls to the staff had been overheard or someone from the press just became suspicious when San's staff all over the island began leaving parties abruptly at midnight. Surely that was the explanation. The press didn't really know anything. They were just snooping around, hoping for a story.

But as Karen stepped outside into the glaring lights from the TV trucks, she quickly realized that her assumption had been wrong. The first question about what had malfunctioned at the Sans and how many patients had died made Karen's worst fears come true. Someone had definitely tipped the press, and they knew exactly what was going on inside the Sans. Karen confidently assured the press that no patients had died as she silently prayed that was still true and that Cynthia Charles was still hanging on. She told them that there had been some type of a computer malfunction but that everything was fine now and that the Sans was running manually and without problem. The next question about whether she had sent for some real doctors made Karen see red. "The Sans has competent, qualified staff, and they are managing the patients appropriately. They are doing everything that any doctor could do," she assured them. "Now, I need to get back inside to my patients. Everything is under control here. That is your story," she said as she turned to go back into the Sans. The reporters all called out questions as she made her hasty exit. Even as she ignored them, she had a bad feeling that this was going to be played out in the press as the New Year's Day headline. She braced herself for the onslaught that was sure to come.

A few minutes later, she received word that Senator Charles had arrived and was demanding to see her in his wife's room. She could hear him shouting at the staff as she neared the room. The words *incompetent* and *lawsuit* came out loud and clear. When she entered the room, she could see that the Senator was totally out of control. He ran toward her, shaking his fist in her face as he spat out, "If my wife dies, I will hold you totally responsible. This is a farce. You and your staff are incompetent. I want a doctor, and I want one now, or I will personally have this place closed down."

The door opened and Ted appeared, wearing a white lab coat. "Maybe I can help you, Senator. I am *Doctor* Ted Richards." The senator looked confused but accepted Ted's extended hand. "If you want, I will assist the staff with your wife's care." The senator found his voice and said, "Are you a real medical doctor? I don't want any fancy nurses or PhDs in here."

Ted assured the senator that he was a real doctor with a real medical degree from a real US medical school. The senator accepted that and walked into the adjoining suite and sat down heavily. "Please help her," he pleaded. "I can't lose her now. She was just starting to feel better."

Ted put his hand on the Senator's shoulder and looked down at him. He assured the senator that he would do his best to help his wife. "Just give us a little time alone with her, and then you can sit with her if you like." Ted closed the door as he walked back to the bedside. Helen and Tom looked shell shocked, and Karen looked no better. She did manage to introduce Ted to the staff as her old grad school friend. She wasn't sure if she were angry with him or grateful that he had calmed the senator. At this point, she didn't have time to find out. There was just too much to do to control the chaos, and she spent the rest of the night doing just that.

Chapter Twenty-Three

It was worse than she had expected—much worse. "Disaster at the Sans!" was the lead story on New Year's Day worldwide. The AMA was clamoring for the Sans to be closed down immediately. The Sans was a deathtrap, according to them. It was a travesty for anyone to think she could run a hospital without doctors, and this disaster was exactly what Karen and the Sans deserved for trying. Karen held her head and groaned as she listened to the head of the AMA telling the press that Sans Docteur Hospital must close before someone dies. She wondered what had ever made her think she could pull this off. Was she crazy? Before she could make that decision, the buzzer sounded, and her secretary told her that Vice President Gordon was on the phone. Karen was tempted to drop the phone and run, but instead she pushed the flashing button and waited for the onslaught. She was pleasantly surprised when she heard Mel Gordon saying, "Karen, it's Mel. Are you okay? I heard about problems at the Sans shortly after midnight last night. The president is at Camp David so they called me first. What happened?"

Karen gave her a quick briefing on the events at the Sans. Mel was professional but sympathetic as she asked, "Is everything stable now? Any more problems?"

Karen answered honestly, "Everything seems to be fine, but we haven't put the computer system back online. We are still running manually and will continue to do so until we are sure that our system is safe. The main problem is that our computer guru is missing. He called in sick yesterday, and no one can find him now. He just seems to have vanished. I can't imagine where he could be that he hasn't heard about our problems. It's really strange."

The vice president said that she would brief the president and try to keep things under control from her end. She hung up after making Karen promise to let her know if anything else happened at the Sans.

Karen was so glad that today was Friday, and she would not have to make the decision about canceling surgeries until Sunday. She knew that if they had not identified the source of the computer glitch by then she would have no choice but to cancel. She could not allow patients to undergo computer-driven robotic surgeries with malfunctioning computers. Their robotic surgery was one of the modalities that had made Sans Docteur unique. Sure other hospitals used robots, but they were driven by fading surgeons whose hands were no longer sure and steady enough to perform intricate surgery unassisted. At the Sans, the robots were driven by sophisticated computer programs that were fed landmarks and locations by digital images from the patient's MRIs, CTs, and PET scans. It was foolproof. The robotic hands never faltered as long as the computers were feeding them accurate information. She didn't even want to think what could happen if someone corrupted the data that was being fed to them. It would be too terrible to conceive. But that type of corruption was impossible. The Sans had the most sophisticated security system in the world. Only two employees had top security levels, Carl and Dr. D., and they were certainly beyond suspicion. Weren't they?

Before she could decide, Carl burst into the office. He was waving a letter on the familiar Sans letterhead. "You won't believe it. He's gone. He was sick of working here and decided to leave. He hopes we won't have too much trouble getting a replacement. A replacement on New Year's weekend, in Bermuda, in the middle of this fiasco! What the hell are we going to do?"

Karen grabbed the letter and read for herself that Carl was right. Dr. D. was gone. She turned to Carl and took him by the shoulders. "Carl, please listen to me. I think Dr. D. did something to the computers before he left. This can't be a coincidence. You must find out what he did and correct it."

Carl started to shake his head in denial before he realized that Karen was right. This had to be Dr. D.'s handy work. No one else would have had the expertise or the opportunity to tamper with the system. The shock of the full extent of that realization hit him all at once, and he slumped into the nearest chair and put his head into his hands. "Karen, this is the end. We must close down immediately. I can't fix this. Dr. D. was a genius. I can't begin to compete with him. You know that."

Karen disagreed, "Carl, don't say that. You are the man who invented automated medication administration and computer-guided robotic surgery. You are ten times better than Dr. D. will ever be. Pull yourself together, and get out there. You know what needs to be done, so go do it." As she spoke she took Carl's hands, pulled him from his seat, and led him to the door. "I'll stop by for an update as soon as I finish up here," she said as she shoved him through and slammed the door behind him. Immediately slumping against the door Karen realized that she was shaking and on the verge of tears. She knew that she couldn't afford to fall apart now. She had to hold it together for everyone's sake, but the thought that Dr. D. could have deliberately risked the lives of all these patients was sickening. Why? Why would he do such a horrible thing? And what if Mrs. Charles died? He would be a murderer! And Karen and Sans Docteur would be ruined.

She quickly called for Ted and Barbara and John Geraci. She needed her chief nursing officer and her chief operating officer to help her make sense of this mess. Besides, these were the only people that she was sure she could still trust. Betrayed by one of her own, she no longer trusted her staff. She still hoped she could trust Carl, but, just in case, she would have John keep an eye on him. In addition to his operations experience, John also had extensive expertise as a hospital CIO. He would know if Carl tried anything funny with the computers.

As she briefed the incredulous trio, Karen's confidence started to return. Minutes after filling them in on the details and outlining her plan, Karen had both John and Barbara on their way to the master computer control room. Ted stayed to fill Karen in on Cynthia Charles's condition, which was still grave and getting worse by the minute. "I don't know what's wrong. She should be awake by now, but she seems to be slipping deeper and deeper into coma. I think we are going to lose her if we don't figure this out in the next hour. She can't last much longer."

Karen's eyes filled with tears. She knew what it would mean to the Sans if Senator Charles's wife died but, even more importantly, she liked and cared about Cynthia Charles. Cynthia was a wonderful woman who had already endured more than her share of suffering, and this should not be happening to her. When the operator announced code blue in the VIP Oncology Suite, Karen knew it was Cynthia. Wordlessly, both Karen and Ted ran from the room and didn't stop until they arrived, breathless and scared, at Cynthia's bedside. The code team was already there and working on Cynthia. The senator was looking on from the door of his suite and was obviously in shock. As the team performed CPR, Barbara readied the cardiac paddles. She called "All clear" and shocked Cynthia once. Miraculously, the monitor started to beep with a slow, steady rhythm. Helen, the chief ARNP, gave orders to restart Cynthia's IV, which had come out during the code. She also ordered the usual post cardiac arrest drugs. No one spoke. They quietly went about their tasks. The only sounds in the room came from the regular hiss of the respirator and the beeping of the cardiac monitor.

Karen looked at the medication pump standing against the wall. It was still connected to the computer line and was still pumping out medication. "Why is this still hooked up to the computer? I thought I told everyone to go manual until the glitch was found and isolated?" Karen looked at the young RN who was taking primary care of Cynthia.

"I'm sorry, Karen. I didn't think I needed to disconnect it. The computer console is shut off so it's not controlling the pump."

Karen walked over the computer console and indeed the switch was turned to the off mode and the lights were off, but when she put her ear to the console, she could hear computer noises coming from inside. "Quick, get Carl down here and tell him to bring some tools," Karen shouted as she disconnected the pump from the computer.

Carl was amazed when he opened the console and found it fully operational. The on/off switch and the setting dials were connected on the inside of the console but obviously were inoperative when it came to controlling the computer. The main computer was still controlling the pump. Karen picked up the phone and asked the operator to put her on speaker. Karen's voice could be heard all over the hospital as she calmly instructed the staff to *completely* disconnect all pumps and monitors from the main computer. She announced that this was a test of the down-time procedures and that she would let them know when they should reconnect. There were questioning looks on the faces of the staff, but they followed Karen's direction immediately.

A few minutes later, Karen watched as Helen examined Cynthia carefully. When the ARNP lifted the patient's eyelid as part of a neuro exam, the lids started to flutter, and the patient started to move her arms. Before anyone could react, Cynthia's weak voice demanded to know what had happened and why everyone was staring at her. Karen just reached down and took her hand. The senator was at her side instantly, hugging his wife and crying while he explained that he had almost lost her. He was laughing and crying at the same time. Karen signaled the rest of the team to give them some privacy as she and Ted left the room.

Chapter Twenty-Four

Back in her office, Karen dropped into her chair in complete exhaustion. She knew that the patients were all safe for now, but she also knew that if the computer system was not back online soon, she would be forced to transfer the patients to other facilities and close down the Sans. If they closed down now, the Sans would never reopen and Karen would be a complete and total failure. But even worse, patients would never again experience the kind of caring atmosphere that had prevailed at the Sans. They would forever be doomed to submit to the uncaring world of physician-dominated hospitals.

She desperately tried to think of something she could do, but she was too tired to think clearly. Realizing her need for fresh air, a shower, and some clean clothes, Karen decided to take this early morning lull to go home and shower and pack clothes for the next several days. Once this weekend was over and everyone was back to business as usual, she would be barraged. The AMA, the Bermuda officials, the patients' families, and the press would be ruthless in their demands for explanations. Her enemies would spur them on until the Sans was ruined.

Ted offered to go back to the house with her, but, recognizing that she needed some time alone to think, Karen asked him to stay at the Sans in case the senator needed him. Promising to pick up his suitcase and his toiletries in addition to her own, she smiled and kissed him lightly on the cheek. A cold wind chilled the air, but before she pulled away from the curb, she put the car's convertible top down anyway. She really needed the fresh air to clear her mind. Someone had tried to ruin the one thing in life that she really cared about and believed in, the Sans. For all she knew at this point they might have already succeeded. There was no way to predict the reaction the public would have when they heard about this on the morning news. Would anyone ever trust the Sans again? Or, would they return to the physicians' treatment that they had trusted and felt comfortable with for so many generations? She wished she knew. Just as she wished she knew what to do about Ted. Her feelings for him were becoming too strong to deny. She loved him, and sooner or later she would have to face that fact and make some difficult decisions about her future. She was starting to feel a little better as she thought about her feelings for Ted and crossed the causeway. Suddenly she saw something lying in the dark road ahead of her. She cursed under her breath as she slowed to a stop. As soon as she put the car into park and reached for the door handle, someone grabbed her shoulder from behind. The touch made her blood run cold and her heart beat so hard that she thought it would jump out of her chest. She felt as though she were going to faint when a deep voice told her to stay still. Before she could turn toward the voice, a cloth cover her mouth and nose. She tried to scream, but the force was too strong; she found that she couldn't make a sound. Her last thought was of Ted as she felt her consciousness slip away into an eerie blackness, darker than anything she had ever experienced.

Slowly emerging from the darkness, Karen was afraid to open her eyes. She believed that she was dead and fully expected to see the bright light and the stream that everyone describes in their near-death experiences. Holding her breath and squeezing her eyes shut, Karen avoided her moment of reckoning as long as possible.

Finally unable to stay still any longer, she slowly opened her eyes and tried to focus on the surroundings. She was no longer in her car or on the dark road. This was her bedroom, and she was in her own bed. For a moment she thought that she had dreamt all of this and that everything was fine. But then she caught sight of the well-dressed man sitting in a chair next to her bed holding a paper in his one hand and a pharmacy bottle in the other. He stared down at her, and his eyes were as black and as cold as the devil himself. A cold shiver ran down her spine as he spoke to her.

"Welcome back," he said. "You certainly took your time waking up. I didn't give you that much ether. I was really getting tired of waiting for you."

Karen tried to sit up, but he shoved her back down roughly. "You are not going anywhere. Just stay where you are, and do exactly what I tell you, and I might make this easy on you. Otherwise, you're gonna wish you were already dead."

Karen didn't miss the implication as she sank back down on the bed. Her right hand automatically reached out as he handed her a sheet of paper. When her eyes finally focused on the page, the message was short and simple. It was a suicide note from Karen stating that the Sans was a failure and that Karen realized that there could never be a hospital without doctors. It was an idiotic dream. Karen was sorry but she couldn't live with the failure. She apologized to Robert and told him that she loved him and that he shouldn't mourn her. He should find someone new and start over. She couldn't go on but he should. This was her failure, and not his. She was ending her life here and now.

What a neat package. It tied up all of the loose ends. Karen looked up at the man and shook her head. "I'm not going to sign this. This is crazy." She started to get up, and the man shoved her back again.

"You will sign it," he said. "If you don't, patients will start to die. One an hour will die until you sign, starting now." He looked at his watch and dialed his cell phone. He instructed the person on the other end to kill the first patient. Unable to stand the thought of patients dying, Karen begged him to stop and said she would sign the paper. He handed her a pen and a book to support the paper for her signature. Karen looked up at him with tears in her eyes, but he simply pointed to the paper and told her to sign. Signing blindly, Karen wondered what would happen to her now. She didn't have long to wait. The man took the signed paper, folded it, and put it into his jacket pocket. Her heart sank as she realized that he was wearing black-leather driving gloves and there would be no finger prints but hers.

The man handed her a bottle of Alice White Chardonnay. He ordered her to pour herself a glass. She poured the wine, wondering what would come next. He then handed her the pharmacy bottle. She noticed that it was a strong sedative and that the name of the patient on the label was Karen Jorgensen. They really had thought of everything.

He told her to take the pills, all of the pills. Karen shook her head and rolled away from him. Again, he pushed her back. "I'm not playing anymore. Start taking those pills, or the first patient will die."

Karen could tell by the hard look in his eyes that he meant it. She picked up the glass with shaking hands and took the first pill. The man took the bottle from her and held her wrist tightly as he shook out a bunch of pills into her open hand. "Take them all," he ordered.

Karen knew that she was going to die as she took all of the pills in her hand and swallowed them with the rest of the wine. Pouring another glass he shook the remainder of the pills into her hand. Closing her eyes and swallowing the rest of the pills, Karen finished the Chardonnay, thinking that it was ironic that she would die drinking her favorite wine.

Within minutes, Karen started to feel drowsy. Her head and her eyelids were so heavy. She fought the feeling, but it was useless. As her head fell to the side, and she started to snore softly her last thoughts were of Ted. She realized that she had loved him all along. If only she had told him.

Just as Karen was about to give up all hope of surviving, she heard a commotion in the room. Forcing her eyes open she saw the man fall over as someone hit him on the head from behind. Her eyes were too heavy and as they closed, she heard someone calling her name from far away. Then there was nothing but darkness and silence.

Chapter Twenty-Five

Karen heard someone calling her name again. It sounded so far, far away. Wanting to resist, she somehow knew that she had to answer. As consciousness returned, Karen was afraid to open her eyes. If the man noticed she was awake, he would make her take more pills, but she couldn't do it. She was already too dizzy and nauseous. She couldn't drink anymore without vomiting, and she knew that would make him very mad.

As much as Karen didn't want the man to know that she was awake, she could no longer bear to keep her eyes closed. Opening them slowly, her eyes focused on the room, and she suddenly realized that she was no longer in her bedroom. She was somewhere else. It looked like a hospital room at the Sans, and Barbara and Helen were looking down at her and smiling. Someone was holding her hand and squeezing. She smiled up expecting to see Ted. But, it wasn't Ted. It was Robert, and he was speaking to her. "Thank God, you're back. I thought I had lost you," he said in a shaky voice, as he leaned over and kissed her lightly on the forehead.

Allowing her eyes to close, Karen instantly fell back into a sound sleep. Her dreams brought her back to her bedroom and the man who wanted to kill her. But this time Ted had come, and Ted had saved her. She had known that he would come. He loved her, and she loved him. It was time to tell him. In her dream, Ted gathered her up into his arms and kissed her passionately. She told him over and over that she loved him as she clung to him and kissed him back with the same passion. The two were just about to make love when she awoke.

It was several hours later and the room was dark with the beeping of the cardiac monitor as the only sound. As she stirred, someone rose from the chair next to her bed. She called Ted's name, but as the figure came closer, she saw that it was not Ted. It was Robert. She was confused. Where was Ted? Why was Robert here? Had someone called him? Had Ted called him? She didn't think so, but here he was. He came to her with a glass of water and helped her to raise her head and take a sip. As he lowered her head back to the pillow, she looked into his eyes and was surprised to see that he had been crying and was obviously in need of sleep. His normally perfect hair was rumpled, and his clothes were wrinkled and smelled lightly of perspiration. His usual clean citrus scent was missing. This was not the Robert she knew, and she wondered what had happened to him. Surely the flight over to Bermuda had not caused this change. He always flew first class and carried a fresh shirt to change into before landing. She stared at him and was just about to ask him what was wrong when the door flew open, and Barbara came in.

"Boy, are you one lucky lady. If Robert had been ten minutes later in coming to your rescue, you wouldn't be here. He saved your life."

Karen looked from Barbara to Robert and shook her head. This wasn't right. They were confused. It was Ted who had saved her. Barbara laughed and sat down at the side of the bed and took Karen's hand. "Sweetie, do you remember anything from last night?" she asked.

Karen's throat was sore, and it was difficult to speak. She finally managed to say, "The man…he tried to kill me. He made me take the pills and sign the letter. Why? Why did he want to kill me?" she pleaded, with tears streaming down her face.

"The police think that someone hired him to kill you and make it look like suicide. The letter said that you couldn't bear the failure of the Sans. They think that the same people who caused all the trouble at the Sans hired the killer," Barbara explained.

"But who? Who would want to ruin the Sans and kill me?" Karen demanded.

Robert came to the other side of the bed and touched her face as he explained, "Karen, you know how many people back in the States hate you and hate the Sans for what it represents. You can't go against the entire medical community and not make enemies. I warned you. You know I did. I told you to give up this foolishness before it caused trouble. You just wouldn't listen. You had to have your precious hospital, and this is the result. If I hadn't finished my business trip early and decided to surprise you, I don't know what would have happened. When I arrived home, I heard the man in our bedroom ordering you to take the pills. I didn't know what to do. I couldn't take the chance of going back out to call the police so I used the phone in the living room to dial 911. I didn't even wait for an answer. I left the phone on the couch and picked up a golf club from my bag. The man turned toward me just in time to see a golf club crashing down on his head. I didn't mean to hit him that hard. I didn't want to kill him. I just wanted to stop him from hurting you," Robert pleaded. "I picked you up, put you into my car, and raced to the Sans. I ran through the front door, screaming for help. Everyone came running, and they took you away. I don't know what happened then, but a few minutes later, Barbara came out and took me to the ICU. The staff was pumping your stomach. You were already attached to monitors and receiving IV medications. They told me that I had saved your life. Just a few minutes more and you would have been gone." Robert's voice failed as he finished. He put his face into his hands and cried.

In truth, Robert was supposed to arrive home and find Karen dead from an overdose of pills with the suicide note on his pillow. By arriving home too early, he had walked in on the actual murder in progress. He didn't know what to do until he realized that he couldn't go through with the plan to kill Karen. As much as he wanted the Sans to fail and as much as he wanted his freedom to be with Tina and William, he couldn't be involved in Karen's murder. He knew that the killer would not stop on his command. He didn't know that Robert was actually the one who had hired and paid him. If Robert tried to interfere, the killer would probably find a way to kill him, too. In desperation, Robert entered the room and brought the golf club down on the man's head with as much strength as he could muster. He knew that the man must die, because if he lived, he might tell the police the story that would lead them to Robert's partners and eventually to Robert himself. No, the killer could not live. Robert had to make sure of that, and he did. He hit the killer with all his might. He felt the skull give way and heard the sickly thud as the club bounced off the killer's head. He was about to hit him again when Robert realized that the killer was dead. He was slumped on the floor with an ever-widening circle of blood gathering around him. Robert knew that no one could lose that much blood and live, and he felt immediate relief.

Shaking uncontrollably, Robert stopped himself from making the second blow. He realized that with the killer dead, no one would blame him. He would be hailed as a hero who had risked his life to save his wife. No one would ever guess that Robert had been involved in this conspiracy from the beginning.

But now that it was over, what was he going to do about Tina? He had promised her that he was going to tell Karen that he wanted a divorce. It had been easy to promise what he believed would never happen. Instead, Karen would be dead, Robert would be a widower, and Tina would be happy knowing that even if Karen hadn't died, Robert would have left her anyway. It would have been perfect. But now what? His plan was ruined, and Tina would be furious. He had to think. How could he make this right with Tina? He would have to appeal to her motherly emotions. She couldn't expect him to tell Karen that he wanted a divorce while she was still in such a frail state. Karen had almost died. He would have to wait until she recovered both her mental and her physical health. Tina would understand that, and it would buy him some time to think and plan. Right now he had worse problems. What would the partners say when they found out that Robert had saved Karen? Robert knew that he wouldn't have a second chance to make it right with them. He would have to placate them somehow. If that failed, he knew that he would be the next on their hit list, and he would need to take Tina and William and disappear. Realizing what a precarious position he was now in, Robert cried even harder. How had he gotten himself into such a mess?

Chapter Twenty-Six

Carl and the rest of the HIS staff had been working around the clock and had finally discovered the cloaked program. Carl was amazed. This was genius. No one on the HIS team had realized that there were actually two distinct systems. All of the real work was going on behind the scenes in the cloaked system while the front-line system only appeared to be in control. The cloaked system was where the commands that had almost destroyed the Sans and taken the lives of many patients had been hidden. Carl realized immediately that there was only one person with enough genius to create such a program: Dr. D.! That's why Dr. D. had resigned so mysteriously and so suddenly. But even now, Carl couldn't believe that Dr. D. had been willing to kill patients. Dr. D. was a medical doctor as well as a computer genius. How could a doctor bring himself to kill patients? Only Dr. D. knew the answer.

Actually, Dr. D. had lost his medical license in the States many years ago when his negligence had caused the death of several patients. The credentials that he had provided to the Sans were bogus, but the partners had made sure that they were impeccable. In fact, they belonged to an excellent physician who had made the mistake of criticizing the partners in public. That physician had taken a long vacation to France and had never returned. He would never return. The partners had seen to that just in time to provide his credentials to Dr. D. At one time, Dr. D. had actually been a fairly competent physician, but that was long before he had succumbed to his addition to drugs and gambling. When his gambling debts climbed into the millions, he became desperate. He knew that he had no choice when the partners called on him to sabotage the Sans.

Dr. D. did exactly as he was instructed up until the last minute. Guessing that the partners wouldn't trust him to keep his silence once his job was done, Dr. D. knew that he had to disappear or die. As soon as he had placed the final command into the cloaked system, he donned a disguise and headed for the airport. By the time all hell had let loose at the Sans, Dr. D. was on his way to Italy. His false passport and his new look guaranteed that he would not be tracked. He would be free to spend the rest of his life in luxury, spending the two million dollars that the partners had paid him in advance. They thought that he had used the money to pay his gambling debts, but he had actually deposited it into a numbered Swiss account that he intended to access from the safety of Italy.

As Dr. D. landed in Italy, the partners were eagerly watching CNN for news of the disaster at the Sans and the unfortunate death of its founder and CEO, Karen Jorgensen. Instead, they learned of Karen's last-minute rescue by her loving husband, Robert. They couldn't believe what they were hearing. Robert had crossed them. But why? He had hated the Sans and Karen even more than they did.

When the news of Dr. D. and the cloaked computer information system broke, the partners went berserk. All their time, planning, and money had been wasted. The Sans was exonerated, Karen was very much alive, and Robert was a hero. The senior partner picked up the phone and hit number one on the speed dial. "Pick up Robert Jorgensen and Dr. D. I want to see them here now!" he screamed into the phone, before throwing it across the room where it smashed into the wall and broke into pieces.

Chapter Twenty-Seven

Ted had been at the Sans when Robert brought Karen in. His own heart had almost stopped when he saw that she was unconscious. He had wanted to grab her from Robert and shove him out of the way. What was he doing back anyway? There was something wrong here. Ted didn't like or trust this man. He knew that Robert didn't really love Karen, but he had to admit that Robert had put on quite a show. Robert as the grieving, loving husband and the hero was more than Ted could stand. Later, when Ted tried to see Karen, Robert turned him away, saying that Karen needed to rest and that he would tell her that Ted had stopped by. When he suggested that Ted should get back to his patients, Ted had almost hit him. Instead, Ted turned on his heels and left the Sans. He called a cab and headed for the airport and didn't stop until he was back in his house in Seattle. Feeling exhausted, he poured himself a double scotch and sat down on his couch. It was going to take a lot more scotch to shield him from the mental picture of Karen and Robert together back in their bedroom in Bermuda. He took the phone off the hook and downed the first of what would be many shots of scotch. As he sank into despair, Karen was distraught. Barbara was telling her that Ted was gone, and Robert was telling her that it was just as well. She needed to rest when they went home, and it was not a good time to be entertaining guests. Karen heard their voices but refused to believe that Ted had left her. Didn't he love her? How could he leave her now when she had almost died? Didn't he care? As she started to cry, Robert asked Barbara to get her a sedative. "She's just over emotional right now. Can you give her something before I take her home?" he asked. Barbara had an uneasy feeling. She didn't trust Robert, but he was right. Karen needed something to calm her down before she could be discharged home. Her suggestion that Karen and Robert stay at her cottage with her and John had been bluntly refused by Robert, saying that Karen would recover faster in her own house. Barbara had argued and lost. Robert was the husband, and it would be his way.

Giving Karen one more hug, Barbara closed the door to Robert's car. "Call me later so I know that you're okay," she instructed Karen. Robert smiled and told her that Karen would need her rest and would not be talking on the phone for at least a few days. As he drove away, Barbara and John stood looking on in frustration. Neither of them trusted Robert, but there was nothing they could do. They both agreed that they would stop by and see Karen tomorrow whether Robert liked it or not.

Karen regained her physical strength incredibly fast. Her mental strength was another story. She felt profoundly depressed as an overwhelming sense of loss spread over her. She missed Ted so much, but she felt as though he was lost to her forever. He had deserted her just when she had needed him the most and she could never forgive him for that.

Robert fussed over her for the first few days after she returned from the hospital. It was almost like the first months of their marriage, and Karen was completely fooled. She felt that Robert loved her and that she owed it to him and their marriage to forget Ted and concentrate on him.

It was the third day home when she walked in on Robert talking quietly on the phone. He was telling someone that he would see them tomorrow. When he looked up and saw Karen, he immediately said that he had to go and hung up. He looked at Karen sheepishly and took her hand. "I'm afraid that I must get back to work. I would love to take you with me, but I don't think you're up to traveling yet. It's best if you recover here. Do you want me to hire a nurse to take care of you?"

Karen was profoundly disappointed. She thought that Robert was going to stay awhile so that they could start to work things out with their marriage. She had hoped that they could put the last few years behind them and return to the relationship they had shared during their first years together. It surprised her how much she wanted Robert to stay, but she knew better than to try to persuade him. Whenever Robert made up his mind to do something, he did it. No amount of begging would sway him. She simply said, "I'll be fine. Don't worry about me. I'm going back to work tomorrow, too."

Robert left the next morning without even waking Karen to say good-bye. As he stood looking down at her sleeping, he had the feeling that he would never see her again, and it saddened him. As much as he wanted to be with Tina, he still had strong feelings for Karen. He would miss her. He kissed her lightly on the cheek and left the room quickly before he could change his mind.

Karen didn't go to work that morning. Depression had set in for real, and she just couldn't bring herself to get dressed and leave the house. Instead, she spent hours walking on the beach and wondering where she had gone wrong. Was the Sans a mistake? Should she just walk away and go back to the States with Robert? She just couldn't decide. Her confidence was gone, and she just wanted to crawl back under the covers and hide.

Chapter Twenty-Eight

On the other side of the States, Ted was feeling the same way. He couldn't bring himself to return to his office and his patients. His practice, which had once been the most important thing in the world to him, was now meaningless. New patients came and went in an endless stream as the HMOs made their whimsical changes in contracts and benefits. In the old days, Ted's patients were as loyal to him as he to them. But now they had no choice. They had to follow the directives of whichever HMO their companies chose. It was definitely "healthcare du jour," and Ted hated it. He couldn't do his job this way. By the time he was familiar with a patient and could make suggestions for improving the patient's health, the patient would call to tell him that he was in a new HMO and had to pick a new primary care physician. Some of the patients were upset and tried in vain to fight the changes, but most simply went along like cattle to the slaughter. In the long run, the HMOs always won. The patients went without any preventative healthcare, showing up in the ER when some preventable disease had reached the point that the patient could no longer function. By this time, it was usually too late to do anything curative. It was simply a matter of managing the worst symptoms until the patient died. *Welcome to healthcare in the twenty-first century in the most affluent country in the world*, Ted thought sarcastically.

Ted made up his mind. He was going to close his practice in Seattle. Brian Wills, the young physician who had been covering for him, had told him many times that he would love to take over permanently. Ted would call Brian and ask him to make an offer. Ted really didn't care how much he offered. The money wasn't important. Ted's sense of integrity and peace of mind was.

As it turned out, Ted had been right. Brian was ecstatic. Obviously, he had been expecting Ted's departure and made a generous offer on the spot. Accepting without hesitation, Ted told Brian that he would not be returning to the office and that he would appreciate it if Brian had the papers drawn up right away. Brian agreed, saying that he would have them couriered to Ted by the end of the week.

Even Ted was impressed when the papers arrived the next morning. Brian certainly worked fast. He was not giving Ted any option for changing his mind. Ted asked the courier to wait while he signed the papers and wrote a note to Brian. In the note, he asked Brian to have all of his personal belongings boxed and sent to storage. He told Brian that he would be taking an extended vacation and wouldn't need them for quite awhile. In closing, Ted thanked Brian and wished him well with the practice.

Experiencing an overwhelming sense of loss, Ted packed his suitcase and headed for the airport. A message left for his housekeeper instructed her to close up the apartment and to expect a generous bonus in her next paycheck. Right now he didn't want to speak to anyone. He just wanted to get away.

When the taxi dropped him at the airport, Ted just wandered around, not knowing where to go. Noticing the sign for Air Italia, he made a decision. Remembering that he had always wanted to see Tuscany, he walked up to the counter and asked for a one-way, first-class ticket to Rome. He would rent a car there and drive through Italy. It would be a great escape. He had never been to Italy and there would be no unwanted memories there to haunt him.

The girl at the ticket counter questioned the one-way ticket, but Ted assured her that he was going on an extended vacation and didn't yet know where he would go after Italy. Satisfied with that explanation, she printed out his ticket and wished him a nice trip.

Ordering his third scotch, Ted sat in the terminal bar, waiting impatiently for his flight to be called. He was on his feet at the first boarding announcement. Throwing a twenty on the bar, he grabbed his flight bag, and practically ran for the gate. His first-class ticket assured his right to board first, and he intended to take full advantage of it. As he pushed ahead of everyone, he remained totally unaware of the curious looks from the passengers and attendants. Taking his seat by the window, he immediately rang for the flight attendant and ordered a double scotch.

By the time the jet touched down in Rome, Ted had downed several doubles and was feeling no pain. After clearing customs, he took a cab to a nearby hotel and slept for almost twenty-four hours. Awakening in the dark, he looked out the window at the lights glowing down below, his heart skipping a beat as he immediately thought of Karen and how much he wished she were here to enjoy this sight with him. Shaking his head in disgust Ted realized that he had flown halfway around the world to get away from her and here she was with him anyway. He picked up the phone and called room service, knowing that a nice bottle of twenty-year-old scotch would certainly help him get Karen off his mind.

Back in Bermuda, Karen was feeling only slightly better on Monday morning. She had resigned herself to the fact that Ted was gone. He didn't love her and she had to accept that and get on with her life at the Sans. The most important thing now was for the Sans to survive and flourish. It was all she had left to live for.

Later, when she held a press conference, she appeared to all as the epitome of poise and confidence as she assured the press that the Sans had indeed survived Dr. D.'s sabotage. No patients had suffered any permanent ill effects, thanks to the competence of the staff at the Sans. Everything was functioning as it should, and the staff was rescheduling the surgeries that had been postponed. In fact, Karen invited the press to witness one of the computer-driven robotic surgeries firsthand. She assured them that they would be amazed by the efficiency and precision of the robots, which could perform any surgery in half the time it took a human surgeon and with a 0-percent complication rate. No human surgeon could make that boast and live up to it.

George Stafano, the nurse anesthetist, allowed the reporters and photographers to enter the viewing booth above the surgical suite as soon as the patient was anesthetized. Speaking to them through a small microphone embedded in his earpiece, he welcomed them to the world of robotic surgery. As the nurses draped and positioned the patient, the techs wheeled Donatello, the computer-driven robot, into place at the right side of the patient. George showed the press the small computer and explained how it had created the medical plan for the patient, which in this case included surgery. The medications that put the patient into a deep sleep were precisely calculated according to the patient's current health status. Taking into account the patient's age, liver function, renal function, and cardiac function, the computer performed the necessary calculations in seconds. The computer also reviewed all of the digital data from the CT scans, MRIs, and ultrasounds and accurately plotted the exact location of the tumor and surrounding nerves and blood vessels. With astonishing precision, the computer guided the robotic scalpel or laser through the patient's body without hesitation. In fact, in hundreds of trials, Donatello had never made a mistake. No nerve or blood vessel had been unwittingly nicked or severed. No bowel or bladder was accidentally perforated, even in the worst cases of altered anatomy. The computer monitored the patient throughout the surgery and immediately identified and made course corrections for any change in the patient's anatomy or condition.

The reporters were astounded as Donatello finished what would normally be a multi-hour surgery in less than thirty minutes. They couldn't believe their eyes as the robotic hands sutured the wound closed and were even more astonished when Donatello completed a thorough examination of the patient and proceeded to order the removal of the breathing tube from the patient's mouth. The patient coughed briefly and then began breathing normally. He was awake and on his way to the recovery room within one hour of entering the OR.

Karen called their attention to the fact that the patient would normally have been under anesthesia for many hours, and that fact alone could have led to complications in conventional surgery.

The worldwide headlines that night stated simply, "The Sans Survives and Thrives!" and went on to describe the sabotage and the murder attempt and the heroic acts of Robert and the Sans' staff. The press made Robert the man of the hour. He had rescued his wife and had thus assured the future of Sans Docteur Hospital. The newspaper and video accounts of the robotic surgery were so complimentary that there was no doubt in anyone's mind that the Sans was the place to go if you needed any type of surgery and wanted to make 100-hundred-percent sure that it would be done correctly.

The partners and Dr. D., all watching from their separate homes, couldn't have been more furious with Robert. How could he have betrayed them like this? What could he have been thinking? He wanted the Sans destroyed even more than they did. Hating the Sans and blaming it for ruining what was left of his marriage, all Robert wanted was to be free to start his new life with Tina and William. Karen was the only thing standing in his way, and he had just saved her life. It was beyond belief.

The week dragged on, and by Friday rounds, everything seemed to be back to normal at the Sans. Carl and his IT staff had spent endless hours pouring over every line of programming and had discovered dozens of corrupt commands in both the primary and secondary systems. At this point, they were satisfied that they had found all of the aberrant commands and that the system was now clean and reliable. Carl reassured Karen and the board that they could now trust the computers and no longer needed to run manual checks out on the units. In his written report, Carl sounded strong and confident, but Karen was disappointed to find him slumped in his office chair with his hair looking like he had tried to pull it out. Wrinkled clothes and the slight smell of perspiration gave Karen the impression that he hadn't bothered to shower or change clothes in days.

"Carl, what's wrong?" Karen demanded. "You look like crap. When's the last time you took a shower?"

Carl straightened and attempted to push his unruly hair back into place as he avoided looking at Karen. Looking at his shoes instead, he mumbled, "I've been working non-stop, thank you. We have had a few problems, in case you didn't notice."

Karen was shocked by Carl's response. This was totally out of character for a man who was normally polite to a fault and hated sarcasm in any form. Putting one hand on his shoulder and sitting on the desk next to him, she tilted his head up and looked into his eyes. She could see that he had been crying and her heart went out to him. "Carl, what's wrong? Why are you so upset? Everything is fine now. Isn't it?" she asked with more than a little trepidation.

Brushing her hand away, Carl stood up and walked to the other side of the office. "Sure. Everything is just perfect now," he said without conviction. "At least it looks perfect. I can't shake the feeling that we are missing something. It was just too easy. Dr. D. would have been more devious."

"Carl, your imagination is getting the best of you. Dr. D. is just a man and not the genius you make him out to be. You are being paranoid. I have every confidence in you and your team. I'm sure that you have found and corrected all of the problems, but if it makes you feel better, run another repair program over the weekend," Karen assured her friend. "Now, please go home and get some rest. You'll feel much better in the morning." Giving Karen a shaky smile, Carl let her guide him towards the office door. "Okay. I'm going home, but I'll be back in the morning to check the system one more time. I'll call you when I'm through," he promised her as he shuffled through the door.

Karen prayed that Carl was just being over cautious. *Why can't that man get some confidence?* she thought. His self-deprecating personality was starting to make her crazy. She didn't want to replace him as CIO, but she would if he didn't step up soon.

Realizing that she was totally spent, Karen finished her rounds and left instructions with the supervisor to page her immediately should there be any further problems. As she walked slowly to her car, her thoughts went to Ted and she smiled wistfully as she remembered how much he had enjoyed driving the Mercedes. Pushing those thoughts from her mind, she forced herself to think about Robert instead and determined to call him as soon as she reached home.

Her night passed pleasantly enough. After a light dinner and a long walk on the beach, she showered and climbed into her four-poster bed. Remarkably, she fell asleep within minutes, forgetting all about her intention to call Robert. Her sleep was dream-filled and restless, and Karen awoke late the next morning still feeling exhausted. Going through her normal activities on auto pilot, Karen finished breakfast and placed the dishes into the dishwasher. She knew that she should be overjoyed with the turn of events and the ongoing success of the Sans, but a sense of loss kept nagging at her. She felt anxious and restless as she wandered aimlessly from one room to another in her empty house. A walk on the beach would be more productive, but she couldn't bring herself to leave the house. Instead, she brewed a cup of tea and took it to her office, where she set about answering the dozens of messages that overloaded her inbox. Finally, reaching the end of the new messages, she looked up and was surprised to see that the room was dark. It was after ten o'clock, and although she had worked through lunch and dinner, she was not the least bit hungry. Instead, feeling exhausted, Karen decided that she needed a good night's sleep. She entered the master bedroom just as the phone began to ring. She groaned aloud as she reached for the button that would transfer the call to her answering machine, but instead, she amazed herself by saying "hello" into the receiver.

"Karen?" Ted's voice sounded as strong as if he were standing right in front of her. Karen's heart skipped a beat. "I'm in one of the most beautiful cities in the world, and I can't enjoy it because you're not with me."

"Funny," she said, as she pulled a suitcase out of the closet. "I was just thinking the same thing."